Harry compressed his lips into a bloodless line. 'You haven't heard the last of this guy. He's going to keep on killing people.'

'How do you know that?'

Harry looked at the District Attorney in surprise, as though the reason was so obvious it hardly required an explanation.

'Because he likes it, Rothko. He really and truly likes it.'

Warner Bros.
A Kinney Leisure Service
presents

CLINT EASTWOOD

in

DIRTY HARRY

A Malpaso Company Production

Co-Starring
HARRY GUARDINO
RENI SANTONI

ANDY ROBINSON
JOHN LARCH
and
JOHN VERNON
as "The Mayor"

PANAVISION®
TECHNICOLOR®

Executive Producer
Robert Daley

Screenplay by
Harry Julian Fink & R. M. Fink and Dean Reisner

Story by
Harry Julian Fink & R. M. Fink

Produced and Directed by
Don Siegel

DIRTY HARRY

Phillip Rock

Based on a screenplay by
HARRY JULIAN FINK
R. M. FINK
and
DEAN REISNER

From a story by
HARRY JULIAN FINK
and
R. M. FINK

A STAR BOOK
published by
the Paperback Division of
W. H. ALLEN & Co. Ltd.

A Star Book
Published in 1977
by the Paperback Division of
W. H. Allen & Co. Ltd
A Howard and Wyndham Company
44 Hill Street, London WIX 8LB
This edition reprinted 1980

Copyright © R. M. Fink, 1971

Printed in Great Britain by
Hazell Watson & Viney Ltd, Aylesbury, Bucks

ISBN 0 352 30099 x

DIRTY HARRY

I

The wind blew steadily out of the northwest, kicking tiny whitecaps through the Golden Gate. A flotilla of schooners raced the wind past Point Bonita, their bright spinnakers ballooning ahead of them, gaudy patches of color against the green headlands of Marin County. It was a beautiful, gusty afternoon, the wind clearing the haze so that from the roof of the Carlton Tower apartments on Russian Hill the man could see the upper reaches of San Pablo Bay. He could see the sun turning Mount Tamalpais to burnished gold, and he could see the mauve shadows creeping out from Tiburon toward the sun-washed hills of Angel Island and the grim rock-falls of Alcatraz.

The man cared nothing for the view. He stood on the roof in the shadow of the elevator housing, his eyes fixed on the jumble of streets fifteen stories below. He watched traffic inching down Hyde and then turned away and walked to another section of the wide flat roof, slowly, casually, oblivious to the wind that whipped at him, tousling his hair and plastering his thin nylon jacket to his narrow chest. He was a young man, but his thin angular face was pinched and hard and his pale gray eyes held no vestige of youth. The weight of a battered brown suitcase in his right hand dragged his

1

shoulder down, and anyone coming upon him at that moment would have assumed that he was a repairman from the elevator company or a technician come to adjust one of the many TV antennas that dotted the roof. They would have been wrong.

Setting the suitcase at his feet, he leaned against the parapet wall and gazed at the city, his arms folded on the ledge. For a moment his eyes lingered on the pristine shaft of Coit Tower and the jumble of apartment houses that seemed to be crawling up Telegraph Hill like fungus on a rock.

"Pigs," he muttered into the wind, "bunch'a goddamn pigs."

There was no malice in his voice; it was a plain statement of fact, uttered wearily, almost in sadness. He looked away and knelt beside the suitcase, laying it flat, flicking open the side catches and raising the lid. Slowly, reverently, the contents were removed—a blue steel rifle barrel threaded at both ends, a sawed-off wedge of firing chamber and bolt assembly set in a groove of hand-rubbed walnut, a tubular steel stock, a folding bipod, a six-power telescopic sight in a cowhide case— and placed in a neat row on the weather-blistered roofing. Then, with practiced dexterity, the man began to assemble the pieces, screwing the barrel into place, snapping on the stock, attaching the sight, and slipping the end of the barrel through the ring on top of the bipod swivel.

"Beautiful," he whispered, running a hand lovingly over the black steel stock. He looked gravely at the rifle, pondering, then reached into the suitcase and brought out a five-inch length of thick steel tubing that he screwed to the end of the barrel. The silencer jutted out like the tailpipe on a car and gave the assembled rifle a custom look that accentuated its deadliness—a weapon handcrafted for the efficient business of killing.

Cradling the rifle in his arms, he got to his feet and walked to a corner of the roof where he placed the bipod legs on top of the wall. Wedging the stock into his shoulder, he made an adjustment to the scope and then pressed one eye into the soft rubber eyepiece. Cars and people jumped into sharply magnified view, the images bisected by the dark lines of the cross hairs. The man swung the gun in short arcs, up and down, side to side, the weapon moving easily on the bipod swivel. Satisfied, he worked the bolt, easing a round into the chamber, and slowly, almost lovingly, traversed the street below.

A young couple browsed in front of a bookstore, thumbing through a rack of paperbacks. The man had corn-colored hair, shoulder length, curling slightly on the ends. The sight lines toyed with the back of his head and inched down his spine.

"College creep," the man hissed with cold contempt. He shifted the gun slightly and fixed his sight on the young man's companion, a shapeless girl dressed in baggy blue jeans and a loose sweater. Her face was thin and gravely pretty, but the man had no interest in her. He swung sharply away, toward the intersection of Jones and Chestnut. An old man wearing a light raincoat two sizes too large for him stood outside a liquor store, a bottle in a paper sack held close to his chest with both hands. The cross hairs pinned him.

"You wine-soaked old fart," the man said under his breath, squeezing the slack out of the trigger, inching the scope upward until the hairs rested on a bloated, wine-ravaged face. "Be doin' you a favor, wouldn't I? But who the hell would give a damn!"

He jerked back from the scope and rubbed his eye with the palm of his hand. His head ached. It was too bewildering. Too many people . . . too many targets. He wanted time . . . time to think . . . to choose carefully. It was important. No one knew how important it was. It was something that had to be done right or not done at all.

You are characterized by a driving force that overcomes all obstacles. You are capable of passionate devo-

*tion to a cause. You are shrewd, analytical, strong, yet
subtle.*

"Yes," he said. "Goddamn it, yes! No fuckin' bums!
No long-haired creeps!"

He settled back to the rifle, leaning his body comfortably against the wall, swinging the piece north, down the slope of Russian Hill toward Aquatic Park and the beach. He locked onto a foreign sports car turning off Larkin into Bay Street. A redhead was driving, her hair tumbling about her shoulders, moving with the wind. The crosslines held her for a second and then she was gone, the gleaming yellow car swallowed by the traffic stream. The man moved the rifle lazily along the multi-windowed face of the ten-story Pacific Inn between Bay and Francisco, working up toward the roof, scanning the windows but seeing nothing. On the roof, a profusion of red, yellow, and green umbrellas jutting up from the center of white-painted iron tables, dozens of lounge chairs ringing an oval swimming pool, a waiter in a red jacket carrying a tray, a fat old man baring his white paunch to the lowering sun, and a young woman supine on a plastic lounge chair, her bikini-clad body gleaming like oiled copper.

"Jesus," the man whispered. "Sweet Jesus."

He lingered over her, the high-powered optics stroking her flesh, toying with the deep shadow between her breasts, the join of her thighs. He sucked in his breath sharply and then exhaled slowly . . . slowly . . . slowly in a long contented sigh.

> Love . . .
> *You've got me where you want me . . .*
> *pull the strings of my heart . . .*
> *Tease me and torment me . . .*
> *but I'm no good without love.*

The girl sang along with the song, her lips moving soundlessly, a dreamy half smile on her young beautiful face. Her name was Sandra Benson and she was staying

4

in room 814 of the Pacific Inn with a lawyer from Sacramento who was not her husband. She had some plans in that direction, however, and she was thinking about them more than she was thinking about the mindless lyrics that poured from the transistor radio beside her chair. When the song ended and an announcer cut in with a feverish spiel for a Daly City used car dealer, Sandra Benson reached down with one long, neatly manicured hand and shut off the radio. She then sat up and ran both hands across her naked waist and the top of her thighs. Her skin felt tacky, and the suntan lotion that she had been rubbing so generously on her body all afternoon had a stale, sour smell. It was close to four o'clock, a slight nip in the air, but the pool was heated to a comfortable seventy-five degrees and its turquoise brilliance held a promise of warmth and cleanliness. Sandra Benson sprang up and ran toward the pool, her long brown legs flashing.

"Bitch!" the man snapped, losing the girl from the bright circle of the gunsight. He traversed left, moving the rifle too quickly, getting nothing but a blur of color. He steadied the movement, locking in on turquoise waves. A smooth bronze form slid past, cutting through the water like a sleek seal.

"Steady . . . steady," the man whispered. His finger went taut on the trigger, a slow even pull.

Sandra Benson rolled onto her back and floated lazily in the silken water. The elderly man who had been sunning himself all afternoon was sipping on a fresh vodka and tonic and eyeing her over his dark glasses. Sandra Benson was not by nature a tease, but she enjoyed having men ogle her body. She was proud of it, and she wondered idly what her breasts looked like as she drifted across the pool. It was her last thought on earth.

There was no sound of a shot, only a whiplike crack through the still air. The bullet plowed downward through her right armpit, spinning her in the water, and

5

came out just above her left hip. In its searing plunge through her torso it cut the aorta and the hemorrhage was immediate and massive. Sandra Benson died without pain and without sound, her mouth open with shock and surprise as she sank to the bottom of the pool in a cloud of spreading crimson.

Harry Francis Callahan, inspector, Homicide Division, city of San Francisco, tilted his spare frame back in his chair and gazed sullenly at the light fixture above his desk. The fixture was as plain and as functional as an egg carton, emitting just the proper amount of fluorescent light for maximum efficiency. Everything in the large, airy room that was the Homicide Bureau's working center had been designed for such a purpose: efficient desks, efficient files, and efficient men.

Harry Callahan leaned forward with a sigh and gazed numbly at the glut of papers strewn across his desk. The affidavits and crime reports on this desk, one of fourteen in the room, were mute testimony to the awesome case load that threatened to bury the Homicide Division under the creeping glacier of the crime rate. Inspector Callahan fought back an urge to sweep every scrap of paper into a wastebasket, planted his shirt-sleeved arms firmly on the desk, and went back to work.

There was the vexing problem of the Buena Vista Park mugger. There had been thirteen victims in six weeks, all of them elderly men with small pensions or living on welfare. Total take to the mugger a mere seventy-two dollars and twenty-six cents. And for that sum of money the mugger had sent three men to the hospital and one to the morgue. Seven of the old men had given good descriptions of the man who had attacked them, and all of the descriptions tallied. They were after a big, red-haired kid between eighteen and twenty years of age who always wore blue jeans, a blue denim wrangler jacket, and a bright yellow shirt.

Harry Callahan mouthed an obscenity as he shuffled all the reports on the case into one neat pile. A red-haired guy in a cowpoke outfit who never, but *never,* strayed beyond the confines of Buena Vista Avenue and Haight Street should have been picked up within ten minutes of the first attack. But no, life was never that simple. Twelve nice old men slapped silly and one punched to death. Six solid weeks of terror. Everything they needed to know about the bravo except his name, address, and social security number and he was still running wild. His lips curled into a snarl just thinking about it. Under the glow of the fluorescents, his gaunt face took on the appearance of a lean and savage wolf. If the mugger could have seen that face, it would have given him pause.

The telephone purred softly beside his elbow and Harry picked up the receiver, cradling it in the hollow of his shoulder.

"Homicide. Callahan."

It was Sergeant Dixon in Communications. "Thought you were off duty."

"I need the overtime," Harry said.

Dixon chuckled softly. "Sure. Well, I got one. Car eighty-two just called it in—a shooting at the Pacific Inn on Francisco. You want to take it?"

Harry glanced across the room. Inspector Di Georgio was talking on the phone. He would be off duty in thirty-five minutes. On his desk, extravagantly wrapped, was a parcel from Gumps. Di Georgio had been skipping lunch for six months to pay for the contents of that package and tonight was the night he was going to give it to his wife. Harry looked away. There was only one other inspector in the room, Joe Weston, and he was talking quietly to a small, sad-eyed black woman, trying to find out who had hated her son so much that he would punch a knife twenty-six times into the boy's belly.

"I'm elected," Harry said into the phone. "That all you've got on it?"

"That's all," Dixon replied. "There's an ambulance on the way. Should be there before you."

7

"OK." He replaced the phone in its cradle and stood up. He was a tall man, but whip thin. If there was any fat on his body, it was well hidden beneath sinew and gristle. He wore a shoulder holster of dull black leather from which protruded the molded rubber grip of a Smith and Wesson forty-four magnum double-action revolver, a weapon that hung beneath his left armpit like a small cannon. When he put on his suit jacket, the gun made a noticeable bulge in the cloth, but Harry was a man oblivious to such sartorial imperfections. Unlike some of the homicide inspectors who could easily have been mistaken for Montgomery Street stockbrokers, Harry looked just what he was—an overworked cop in a cheap suit.

There was a small, restless crowd standing in front of the Pacific Inn when Harry drove up in his blue, unmarked Plymouth. There were two black and whites parked nose to tail in the circular driveway, but Harry had beaten the ambulance from General Hospital by twenty-seven seconds. He could hear its siren howling up Van Ness as he walked quickly toward the entrance. The crowd knew that something big had taken place but they didn't know what it was and this lack of knowledge made them nervous and vaguely belligerent. One of the patrol car officers was standing in the doorway of the huge motor hotel, legs spread, nightstick in both hands, a crew-cut colossus keeping the world at bay. He seemed grateful at the sight of Harry shouldering his way through the press of civilians.

"Where is it?" Harry asked.

The officer, only three months out of the police academy, removed his right hand from his nightstick long enough to touch his hat brim with military exactness.

"On the roof, Mr. Callahan. Officers Tripoli and Cohn are up there now, sir. I'm waiting for the ambulance."

A ripple of sound raced through the gathering crowd and Harry could hear that one word, *ambulance,* being passed back and forth, the word sounding more ominous with each repetition.

An elderly man reached out of the throng and plucked at Harry's sleeve. "What the hell is going on? What's happening in there?"

Harry brushed past him without answering and went into the lobby. He took the elevator to the roof, driven there by a pasty-faced elevator boy who stared straight ahead as though he had been cast out of gray plaster. The elevator stopped with a jerk that pushed Harry's stomach up to his throat, then the door slid open and he stepped out into a panorama of blue sky and red-tinged water.

Officer Tripoli was waiting for him, his normally cheerful face rigid with anxiety.

"It's a rotten one, Harry," he said tautly. "I can't figure it."

"Don't try," Harry said. He walked to the edge of the pool and stared down at the drifting plumes of scarlet. At the far end of the pool, Officer Cohn, his uniform wet to the knees, knelt beside the body of Sandra Benson who lay with her torso on the coping and her legs in the water. The hole in her side where the bullet had emerged was as big as a man's fist.

"We didn't touch her much," Tripoli said as he followed Harry over to the body. "We could tell she was dead."

"Christ, yes," Harry said quietly. Cohn had closed the girl's eyes and she looked very peaceful. Just a young, startlingly pretty girl sleeping in the afternoon sun. Harry looked away.

There were two other people on the roof—a young Mexican waiter and a stout, elderly man in a terry-cloth robe. Both men were pasty faced with shock and the elderly bather was shaking uncontrollably. Harry walked over to him.

"Better sit down," Harry said.

The man sat, heavily. His eyes looked haunted. "My God. It was awful."

"What was?" Harry asked.

The man stared up at him. "That girl . . . that poor girl . . . My God . . ."

"You saw the shooting, did you?"

"No . . . I mean yes . . *and* no."

Harry waited, saying nothing. The man ran a trembling hand across his brow and made an odd gasping sound as though he were trying to force air into his lungs. "There was no one on the roof except me, the girl swimming, and the waiter. There was no sound of a shot. I mean . . . one second the girl was swimming and the next . . ." His voice ended in a choked wheeze.

"Just take it easy," Harry said.

The man gulped air and continued, his voice a mere whisper. "A snapping sound . . . that was all . . . just a snapping sound and then that lovely girl was rolling in blood . . . sinking. My God, my God." He buried his face in his hands.

Harry walked back to the center of the pool and lay down on the warm flagstone. From that angle nothing showed above the roof's five-foot-high wall except blue sky to the north, west, and east. But to the south he could see the top three stories of the Carlton Tower apartments on Russian Hill.

"Oh, shit," he said with deep feeling.

Harry put in a call to Lieutenant Bressler at Homicide and told him what he thought they were up against. It would take a little time for Bressler to get the warrants to search the apartments on the top three floors of the Carlton Tower, but in the meantime all available black-and-white units would be sent to seal off the area.

Harry was over there four minutes after talking to his chief. He parked his car across the driveway that led down to the subterranean garage, and when the first black and whites came screaming up, he ordered the patrolmen to guard every exit and to stop anyone from entering or leaving the building. At the wide front doors he paused and looked up at the towering structure. Somewhere up there someone had pointed a high-powered rifle and now a girl was dead. It could have been an accident—a kid showing off his dad's war relic, a hunter showing off his new deer rifle, the rifles unloaded, of course. No one *ever* kept a loaded rifle around the house! It could have been something like that, but a nasty little feeling had been growing in Harry's stomach from the moment he had seen Sandra Benson's bloodless corpse. It *could* have been an accident, but he knew in his gut that it wasn't. He had been a cop for nineteen years and he had learned to trust his visceral signs.

"What are all these police doing here?" The manager of the Carlton Tower hurried out from his apartment off the foyer, a small man, very neat and prim, wearing an expensive suit and elevator heels. He looked at Harry and the blue-clothed patrolmen with disdain. They could have been a contingent of hippies from the Hashbury as far as he was concerned.

Harry explained, in his best meet-the-public manner, just what they were doing there, but the manager only glared at him.

"That's nonsense," he spluttered. "No one in *this* building would do a thing like that. My God, we don't even allow pets!"

Harry calmed him down and steered the conversation into a more rational vein. "What's on the roof?"

The little man looked blank. "The roof? Nothing. I mean, just a roof. Ventilators, elevator housing, things like that."

"Locked?"

"Of course."

"Take me up there."

The manager did not like Harry's imperative tone. He was on the verge of objecting to it, but one look at the inspector's bleak face and hard, tired eyes made him think better of it.

They took an elevator to the top floor and then went up a short flight of stairs. There was a door at the top, a heavy door sheathed with tin. It would have taken a crowbar to force that door open—if it had been locked.

The manager looked shocked. "I . . . I always keep it locked."

"Nobody's perfect," Harry said. He stepped ahead of the manager, drawing his gun as he did so. The little man stared at it and pressed himself against the side of the stairwell.

"There . . . there won't be any trouble, will there?"

It was not a question to which Harry could give a positive answer. He went through the doorway gun first, shoving the door wide with his right shoulder, his entire body a hair trigger, a coiled spring as he hit the roof; but he was alone up there. Nothing moved in the long shadows cast by ventilator pipes and TV antennas. He made a slow circuit of the windowless elevator housing. There was a tiny access door at the top of plain iron stairs, but the door was heavily padlocked. Harry holstered the magnum and took a deep breath. The view was magnificent at that time of day, the city bathed in gold, the bay a great curve of purple and dark green, but he did not take the time to enjoy it. He went directly to the north side of the roof and walked slowly beside the wall. Something glinted in the fading sun and Harry bent down to it. Taking a pencil from the inside pocket of his jacket he inserted the point of it in the hollow tip of a brass cartridge case and held it up close to his face. It was a thirty-thirty and the acrid smell of burnt powder was still strong. Harry fished a plain white envelope out of his pocket and shook the shell casing into it. He then made a careful search of the immediate area but could find nothing else. One shot. One death. The killer was a marksman.

He straightened up. Something irritated his peripheral vision, nagged at it. He looked to his left where a cluster of TV poles swayed and creaked in the wind. A piece of paper was impaled on one antenna, fluttering like a handkerchief pinned to a clothesline. Harry removed it, holding it carefully by one edge. The single sheet was covered with letters painstakingly cut from newspapers and magazines. He read the message, taking his time, reading it letter by letter, imprinting the words on his mind:

TO THE CITY OF SAN FRANCISCO
I WILL ENJOY KILLING ONE PERSON EVERY DAY UNTIL YOU PAY ME ONE HUNDRED THOUSAND DOL-LARS. IF YOU AGREE SAY SO WITHIN 48 HOURS IN PERSONAL COLUMN SAN FRANCISCO CHRONICLE AND I WILL SET UP MEETING. IF I DO NOT HEAR FROM YOU IT WILL BE MY NEXT PLEASURE TO KILL A CATHOLIC PRIEST OR A NIGGER.
SCORPIO

Harry folded the note with infinite care and slipped it into his pocket. The setting sun bathed his face with a warm, bronze glow, but he felt only the hard, cold chill of an iron claw.

II

Lieutenant Al Bressler lived by a few simple codes and one of them was Never take a damn thing for granted. He didn't just read the note that Harry placed on his desk, he devoured it, turning it over and over in his big gnarled hands, his heavy square-jawed face lined with thought.

Harry waited patiently, leaning back in one of Bressler's comfortable chairs, chewing on one of Bressler's four-for-a-dollar cigars. Through the tall glass windows in the lieutenant's office, he could see garlands of light on Nob Hill. It was a view he had always admired.

"You check out the dead woman?" Bressler's voice sounded like a baritone's in the bottom of a well.

"There wasn't much to check."

"Run it down for me, anyway."

Harry sighed. He removed the cigar from his mouth and stroked the leaves while he talked. "Name was Sandra Benson, aged twenty-two, secretary for Wilson, Potts and Cudahay, Sacramento stockbrokers. She was on vacation, spending it with a guy named Garrison. Charles Garrison."

"Hunh, hunh." Bressler grunted knowingly.

Harry shook his head. "No *hunh, hunh,* Al. It was a clean affair. No overtones or undertones, just a couple of good-looking people enjoying each other. He was planning to marry her and everyone would've danced at their wedding."

Bressler placed the note on the desk and turned it slowly with a thick finger. "I always look for a motive, Harry."

Harry snorted. "A motive? She was the head of the Mafia, for Christ's sake!"

A nerve pulsed in the side of Bressler's jaw but he said nothing.

Harry leaned forward and rested one hand on the edge of the desk. "The note's for real, Al. Face it. Whoever this Scorpio character is, he wasn't after Sandra Benson—just a body count. He flung a corpse in our faces to prove he's not kidding around. Now, where do we take it from here?"

Bressler slipped the note into an envelope marked OK to Handle in red ink. "We drag the mayor from a campaign dinner. He won't be overjoyed."

"Tough."

"Sure, tough. He's not Civil Service like you, Harry. He has to hustle. Give him his due and try not to be too insulting this time."

"I won't spit on his floor, if that's what you mean."

"Just show a little respect. And you could start by getting a shave. You look like a tramp."

Harry grinned and ran a hand over the stubble on his chin. "Well, you know how it is, Al, they don't call me Dirty Harry for nothing."

It was a nice office, Harry had to admit that—deep piled wool carpet, oak paneling, expensive light fixtures, good prints on the walls, cut crystal ashtrays on walnut end tables. First cabin all the way and it was only the secretary's. The last time he had waited in that office, the secretary had been seated behind her elliptical Danish desk and she had been the only jarring note in the place—a tall, angular, no-nonsense monument to bureaucratic efficiency. She wasn't there tonight, but he was still cooling his heels. Only the last time he had been there, Sam Fleming had been with him to keep him company. Sam hadn't been called on the carpet but he had come anyway.

Hell, what are partners for, Harry?

That was the kind of guy Sam was. Harry grinned at the memory, but it was a bitter smile. He missed Sam's big, comfortable presence. They had been partners for five years and made a good team—and a lucky one. Even the shooting that had put Sam into the hospital for the past three weeks had been lucky. They had been after a freaked-out kid who had been knocking over liquor stores, trying to support an acid habit with a forty-five Colt. The kid had crossed the big line one misty afternoon when he had pumped five shots into a store owner who was a little too slow opening the register. They had caught up with him two days later near Ghirardelli Square, and the kid had turned on them like a rabid dog and had started shooting. One of the slugs had gone into Sam's chest and had come out through his left shoulder blade. A clean drilling that would have killed him if it had been one-tenth of an inch one way or the other.

Lucky.

Lucky Sam Fleming and Dirty Harry. They made a good team.

"You can come in now, Harry." Lieutenant Bressler stood framed in the doorway of the mayor's office. Cigar smoke drifted past him like mist around a statue.

"About time," Harry muttered, getting stiffly to his feet.

"Take it easy," Bressler said through taut lips.

"Yeah, yeah," Harry muttered. He strode into the office, not waiting for his chief. Bressler stood there for a moment, feeling like a doorman, then he trailed Harry into the room.

The mayor rose from behind a desk that was not quite large enough to land a light plane on. He was a

16

tall, imposing man who had made his money in the construction industry before retiring to run for office. He owned no small part of San Mateo County, wore three-hundred-dollar suits, hundred-dollar shoes, and fifty-dollar ties. He was as tanned as a golf pro and as sleek as a seal. The contrast between him and Harry Callahan was startling. He was flanked by the chief of police and two City Hall aides. All of them eyed Harry coolly.

"I understand from Lieutenant Bressler that you're in charge of this case," the mayor said. "What have you been doing so far?"

Harry jerked his head toward the anteroom. "Sitting on my ass out there waiting for you."

"Damn it," Bressler hissed. "That's the mayor you're talking to."

The mayor smiled and his voice was balm. "I'm sorry for the delay, Inspector Callahan, but I had a few things to talk over with the chief. This is a very disturbing matter . . . very disturbing. A thing like this can panic an entire city. I want this person stopped, but my position is quite clear. The city of San Francisco doesn't pay criminals not to commit crimes. Instead we pay the police department. I would like to know from you what's being done *now*—and what will be done within the next thirty-six hours. Fair enough?"

"Of course. At the moment there isn't much that can be done. We've got a dozen people working the night shift in the Identification Bureau. We're running cards on every extortionist, rifle nut, rooftop prowler, peeper, and racial agitator in our files. Starting at dawn, Thursday, fifty officers from the Tactical Squad will go on rooftop surveillance. We'll cover key buildings from North Beach to Russian Hill and keep a special watch around Catholic churches and in black areas. We'll back up the Tac boys with continuous helicopter sky watch and there'll be ten extra black and whites on roving patrol."

The mayor seemed impressed. One of his aides, a thin

young man who looked like a history professor, cleared his throat discreetly.

"I was just wondering, Mr. Callahan, this Scorpio—have you considered the possibility that he may be motivated by astrological inducements? That is to say, the forecasts in magazines and papers?"

Harry smiled wryly. "I thought about that. All I can say is that if he is going by the forecasts he has a black sense of humor." He took a torn scrap of paper out of his pocket. "I tore this out of the evening paper. Advice to Scorpios is as follows, quote . . . Follow every law and regulation that applies to you and you will avoid trouble now. Don't try to force things on others or they will resent it . . . unquote. So much for that, but we'll have an astrologer give us a personality profile on Scorpios just in case there is anything to it."

"Oh, there is," the aide said fervidly. "My wife and I swear by it. I'm a moon child."

"All right, Harlan," the mayor growled. He studied Harry for a long moment. "I'm going to put a message in the *Chronicle* the day after tomorrow. I'll tell Scorpio we're willing to go along with him but that we need time to raise the money."

"You can't play games with this creep," Harry said.

"It'll get us some breathing room."

"No, sir. It'll get us some dead people. If you're going to play post office with this bastard, go all the way. Tell him you have the money and set up a meeting. Let me face the son of a bitch."

The mayor chewed his lip and looked quizzically at Bressler. "Lieutenant, what do you think?"

Bressler passed the buck to the chief.

"I'm against it," the chief said. "Something could turn sour and we'd have a bloodbath on our hands."

The mayor nodded solemnly. "I agree with that. I think you're jumping a little too quick, Callahan. That's a bad habit of yours. I don't want any more trouble like you had last year in the Fillmore district. That's my policy."

Harry forced a smile. "When I see an adult male chasing a woman with intent to commit rape, I shoot him. That's *my* policy."

The mayor bristled, his facade of affability slipping. "Intent? How did you establish that, Callahan? Do you read minds?"

Harry's grin became wolfish. "Well, Your Honor, when I see a naked man running down an alley with a butcher knife and a hard-on, I don't figure he's out collecting for the Red Cross!"

The mayor's even tan took on the color of port wine. Bressler made an odd choking sound, muttered something about having to get back to the office, and steered Harry toward the door. He did not relinquish his grip on Harry's arm until they were in the elevator.

"You're all tact! You talked to that man like he was a Haight Street pusher!"

Harry rubbed the side of his nose with the back of his hand. He did not, to Bressler's annoyance, look in the least abashed.

"Do I tell him how to swing in City Hall? He has his job and I have mine. Hell, I voted for him, but I don't want him on my back. He thinks all detectives are right out of Agatha Christie."

"I don't know what the hell *you're* out of. I've known you for twenty years and you're still a mystery."

"If you want my badge, you can have it." Harry's voice was bone weary.

Lieutenant Alfred J. Bressler shook his head numbly, thinking for a moment of his house in Twin Peaks, his wife, his three kids who liked to see him once in a while, and said, almost in anguish, "Jesus, Harry, all I really want is a twenty-five-hour day. We got a helluva lot of work to do by Thursday morning."

"Don't worry about it. Everything gets done—somehow."

They spent the rest of the night in Bressler's office poring over a large scale map of the city. It was nearly dawn by the time they had marked the buildings they wanted covered and had sketched out a plan for coordinating the entire operation. The Tactical Squad men on roof surveillance would be equipped with walkie-talkies so that if they spotted anything they could call in to the helicopter and the roving squad cars. Everything looked good on paper, and if they had any luck at all they'd get Scorpio the moment he stepped out onto a rooftop—if he did step out onto a roof. They were playing the percentages on that. Most criminals were creatures of habit. If something worked for them one time, they'd follow the same pattern again.

Bressler drained his fifth cup of coffee and looked glumly at the dawn. "Grab a little sleep, Harry. I want you to brief Sergeant Reineke and the Tac boys by ten thirty."

Harry filled his own cup and ignored the directive.

The morning dawned clear, but by nine o'clock a line of thick black cloud sliced in from the northwest and it started to rain. Harry ducked across the street to a barbershop and made up for his lack of a night's sleep by having a shave and a shoeshine. He looked crisp and relaxed when he held his briefing at ten thirty. The burly, elite Tactical Squad officers knew how to work as a team and the briefing was a piece of cake. Harry was feeling pleased with himself when he left the police building at twelve forty-five to drive over the route the patrol cars would follow. He took Columbus Avenue to North Point, and as he cut across Larkin, he began to feel light-headed, making him realize that he had nothing in his stomach except six cups of coffee and two stale crullers. There was a hot dog stand at Larkin and Bay that sold the best kosher dogs in the city. He parked in front of the place and dashed through the pelting rain to the shelter of the stand's awning. The tantalizing odors of frankfurters, sauerkraut, and chili wafted up from the steam tray behind the scarred wood counter. Harry straddled a stool and breathed in the aroma.

"Delicious, Mr. Jaffee—absolutely delicious."

A tiny, bald-headed man grinned at him through the rising steam. "Ain't s'een you around lately, Mr. Callahan. Where ya been keepin' yourself?"

"Oh, here and there, Mr. Jaffee. Here and there."

"You want the usual?"

"Right, and extra heavy on the kraut."

Two intense young men in wasp-waisted suits sat on adjoining stools, nibbling at their hot dogs as though they were canapés.

"I find him aesthetically obtuse," one of the young men was saying, "and dreadfully passé . . . a kind of neo-Orphist with no achromatic tonality at all."

"Oh, marvelous," the other one squeaked. "That's *really* marvelous!"

Harry suppressed a smile and looked away, turning his back to the counter. A pretty young thing wearing a transparent plastic raincoat over her hot pants outfit ran across the street, and Harry watched her long, nylon-flashing legs until she disappeared from view inside the cavernous entranceway of the Pacific Bank building.

Lovely, he mused, very lovely—and not an aesthetically obtuse bone in her entire body.

"Here's your dog, Mr. Callahan."

Harry muttered his thanks and picked up the hot dog from the paper plate at his elbow. He munched on it while watching the afternoon crowd scuttle by.

He never tired of watching people. That he was able to derive enjoyment from such a pastime was the only thing that had kept him from climbing the walls during endless hours spent on stakeouts. There were some detectives who would be chain smoking and chewing their fingernails to the knuckles after eight or nine hours seated in a parked car watching people move in and out of a store, but not Harry. He not only could take the strain but he relished it. It was, to Harry, a living theater—a constantly changing parade. No two people alike, no one gesture quite the same as another.

21

They moved past him now, hurrying through the pelting rain: old people and young, beautiful people, ugly people, kind-faced people, grouches, all sizes, all shapes —moving restlessly by.

Harry chewed on his hot dog and watched them, interested but aloof.

"You look at 'em like they were so many goddamn monkeys in a cage!" Sam used to say.

It appeared that way and Harry never argued the fact. His detachment was legendary and Harry was not a man to tamper with legends.

"Mr. Jaffee," he said quietly, "look across the street and tell me what you see."

Mr. Jaffee peered over the counter. "The bank— lotsa wet people—my friend Silverstein's newsstand. Why?"

"Do you see anyone going into the bank?"

"Yeah—some guy going in now. Why?"

"No reason, Mr. Jaffee. It's just that in the past five minutes approximately sixteen people have gone into the bank but no one has come out."

The little man gave Harry a peculiar look. "That supposed to mean something, Mr. Callahan?"

Harry did not answer. He was looking carefully up and down the street as though searching for something that he felt sure he would find. There were many cars parked across the street, but only one had its motor running. A man sat in it, staring straight ahead, one hand on the wheel.

Harry swallowed the last of his hot dog. "Mr. Jaffee, do you have a phone?"

"Sure." He was stirring a pot of chili, but something in Harry's eyes made him toss the spoon into the sink.

"Call 553-0123. Tell them Inspector Callahan has a hunch that the Pacific Bank at Bay and Larkin is being held up."

"Held up?" Jaffee croaked.

Harry nodded, his eyes on the parked sedan, its

exhaust fumes rising like steam from a kettle. "You got the number?"

Jaffee reeled it off quickly.

"Right. Now get to it and tell 'em to hustle."

Mr. Jaffee ducked into the back of his stand where he kept his canned goods and boxes of buns, his cartons of potato chips, and his telephone. Harry stayed where he was, seated rigidly on the stool, his gaze darting from the Gothic archway of the bank to the car parked forty feet away from it.

One hand on the wheel, Harry thought grimly. The other out of sight, clutching a thirty-eight more than likely, a thirty-eight with a chopped-down barrel so that it could be swung easily in the confines of the car. Harry had three options. He could go into the bank; he could go over to the car; or he could stay where he was and wait for the Tactical Squad to come roaring in like the Marine Corps. Blundering into the bank with a drawn gun was right out of the funny pages, and a casual stroll over to the car could be his last walk on earth if the driver was a local boy who had seen him around. Harry stayed where he was.

A man entered the bank, followed by a tall woman in a fur coat. The heavy glass and bronze doors closed behind them like the doors of a tomb. No one came out.

Harry unbuttoned his coat and rested his right hand loosely, unobtrusively, on the butt of the magnum. To the casual passerby he looked like a man scratching his left armpit.

"Come on, damn it!" he hissed through clenched teeth. There was a station house five blocks away, but it could have been on the far side of the moon for all the good it was at the moment.

Two brightly dressed young women ran through the rain and stopped in the archway of the bank. Harry could hear their laughter clear across the street as they shook the rain from their hair. They looked like two gaudy parrots ruffling their feathers, and when they entered the bank, it was in a whirl, going in side by

23

side through both doors. It was an explosive entrance and all hell broke loose.

The alarm bells went off with a nerve-tingling clang of sound, followed almost instantly by the deep, muffled boom of a shotgun.

"Oh, God!" Harry said. He pushed off from the stool and ran into the street, dodged a taxi, and kept on going. He was halfway to the bank doors when they swung open and two men careened out. Each had an airline flight bag in one hand and a gun in the other. The first one out the door was tall and lean, dressed in a well-cut suit and a black, skinny-brim hat. He held a nickel-plated automatic that he waved in front of him like a baton. The other man was burlier and wore chino pants and a leather jacket. The sawed-off shotgun in his hand still smoked.

"Freeze, punks!" Harry yelled.

Both men skidded to a halt on the rain-slick pavement, the man with the shotgun slipping to one knee. The one with the automatic pivoted on his heels and snap fired in Harry's direction, the shot going high, splitting the air like the crack of a bullwhip.

Harry slapped the butt of the magnum and the big gun popped out of its holster and into his hand. He swung it in a short arc, holding the gun with both hands, straight out in front of him, squeezing the trigger the instant the front sight came in line with the gunman's chest. The man spun on his feet, the shiny automatic flipping out of his hand like a silver coin.

The shotgun exploded and Harry felt a searing jolt of pain in his left leg, as though a dozen white hot needles had been jammed into his thigh. He made a quick swinging movement with the magnum and fired twice, the shots following one another so rapidly they sounded like one report. The man with the shotgun catapulted backward and lay still, a crumpled, bloody bundle at the base of the bank doors.

"Bastard!" Harry breathed harshly.

The high-pitched squeal of rubber burning against

asphalt caused Harry to pivot toward the sound. The black sedan was careening out from the curb. The driver had both hands on the wheel and his face was a pale, taut mask behind the rain-streaked windshield. Harry brought the gun up and shot for the head, not aiming, everything taking place too rapidly for that, just firing through blind instinct and a rage to destroy the thing that was bearing down on him. The heavy slugs slapped into the windshield, spraying glass and destroying the face behind it. The driver died with his foot on the accelerator, his body falling sideways across the seat, the wheel spinning out of his lifeless hands. The big sedan veered sharply toward the curb and slammed into the side of a parked car with a hideous crunch of glass and steel.

And for a moment, there was silence, broken only by the gurgle of escaping water from the sedan's radiator and the labored breathing of Harry Callahan. Then another sound intruded, a soft sound, barely audible, heard not so much by Harry's ears as by his brain—the sound of a man dragging his body across concrete. Harry whirled, gun leveled, freezing the movement of the lean gunman on the sidewalk. The man had one hand pressed to his bleeding side, the other outstretched, fingers touching the handle of the shiny automatic.

Harry's lips curled into a harsh smile. "You been counting?"

The gunman stared at him, eyes glazed with hate. Harry took a step closer, the magnum not wavering.

"Well?" Harry asked softly. "Was it five or was it six? Regulations say five . . . hammer down on an empty . . . only not all of us go by the book."

The gunman's face was waxy and sheened with sweat. His fingers still touched the handle of the automatic but they were as stiff as claws.

"What you have to do," Harry said, "is think about it. I mean, this is a forty-four magnum and it'll turn your head into hash. Now, do you think I fired five or

25

six? And if five, do I keep a live one under the hammer?"

The man licked his lips, eyes riveted on the awesome weapon in Harry's fist.

Harry grinned, almost pleasantly. "It's all up to you. Are you feeling lucky, punk?"

In an anguish of indecision the gunman stared at Harry, then he drew his hand back with glacial slowness. Harry walked over to the sidewalk, pain lacing his thigh at every step, knelt beside the man, and picked up the automatic by the barrel.

"I . . . I got to know . . . mister," the man whispered hoarsely.

Harry slowly raised the big black revolver and pressed the cold barrel to his right temple. He pulled the trigger and the hammer fell with a dull metallic click.

"Six. And you lose," Harry said.

The gunman nodded and turned his head away, closing his eyes to the cold, slanting rain.

Patrolman John Briscoe of the Tactical Squad flipped on the siren as he turned into Van Ness. He was Bobby Unser going up Van Ness, but pure Mario Andretti on the long straightaway to Mercy Hospital. Patrolman Briscoe found speed more than just exhilarating, it was a heady, exotic drug, both spine tingling and sensual. He grinned hugely and glanced at his passenger, but the cold, dyspeptic face of Harry Callahan caused his grin to fade.

"This ain't Daytona," Harry snapped.

"Yes, sir, Mr. Callahan." Briscoe eased his pressure on the gas pedal. "This baby's just built for speed . . . hard to hold back."

"Try," Harry said. He turned his head and glared morosely out the side window. He was soaked to the skin, his leg was on fire from knee to groin, he had just left two men dead, and he was stuck with a cowboy like Johnny Briscoe. He let out a long audible groan.

Mercy Hospital was housed in an antiquated brick

building near the Presidio. It had been built originally as a lying-in hospital for poor women and wayward girls, but since the war, it had served mainly as a clearing house for accident cases and, in recent years, as an emergency station for drug-overdose victims. Its doors were always open to the sick, the injured, the freaked-out, and all the other needy refuse of San Francisco's teeming shore—even damaged police officers.

Harry sat disconsolately on an examining table in one of the criblike cubicles in the emergency wing. Someone was having a bad case of hysterics in the hall and the screaming cut into Harry's spine like the blade of a knife. It finally trailed off into a low whimpering, only to be replaced by bursts of maniacal laughter from some distant recess of the old building. Harry shivered and clamped his jaws on a cigar he had bummed from Patrolman Briscoe. He was grateful when an intern walked briskly into the room, but not grateful enough to admit it.

"About time," he said sourly.

The intern, a thin, tired-faced young man, only grinned. He folded his arms and eyed Harry from head to toe. "They fish you out of the bay?"

Harry snorted and shifted the cigar from one side of his mouth to the other.

"You amaze me, Callahan. You are the most accident-prone individual I have ever met. What is it this time?"

"Buckshot in the leg," Harry muttered.

The intern shook his head in admonishment and made a clucking sound with his tongue. "Wouldn't marry the girl, eh, Harry?"

"You're a wiseass," Harry said.

"Of course, all us Viennese brain surgeons are. It comes with the degree. Well, let's take a look at it." He turned to a dispensary table and picked up a stainless-steel basin and an assortment of instruments.

Harry eyed them dubiously. "What're the scissors for?"

27

"I'm going to cut your trouser leg off."

"Like hell you are. The city gives me a badge but I buy my own suits. These pants can be sewn and cleaned. Just pull 'em off."

The doctor eyed the bloody, ragged patch on Harry's thigh and shook his head doubtfully. "It'll hurt."

Harry set his jaw stoically. "For twenty-nine dollars and ninety-five cents I'm all courage. Go ahead and pull."

The doctor pulled, drawing Harry's pants down to his ankles, relishing the sharp intake of the detective's breath.

"You've got a rotten bedside manner," Harry said through gritted teeth.

"And you've got a rotten leg. I ought to put you upstairs."

Harry shook his head emphatically. "No, doc. Just dig 'em out—*here*."

Muttering something under his breath, the doctor went to work, swabbing the punctured area with antiseptic and spraying the entire thigh with a topical anesthetic before digging out the first pellet with a pair of sharp-pointed tweezers. He examined the pellet critically.

"Who shot you? Doctor Fu Manchu? Looks to me like this has been immersed in a rare mixture of cobra-and-cottonmouth venom. You're a DOA and you don't even know it."

"Don't I just." Harry's tone was bleak.

"You've got a leg like a chicken thief's backside. You're going to be limping for a month."

"Yeah, yeah, yeah. Just get on with it."

The doctor glanced at Harry in exasperation tinged with awe. "Don't worry about it. You'll be back in harness in an hour. But, boy, I hope to hell you're making money at what you do!"

Harry sighed with great weariness. "I'm the richest kid on my block."

The doctor snorted and bent down to his work. Harry

sighed again, removed Patrolman Briscoe's ten-cent cigar from the corner of his mouth, flicked a quarter of an inch of cold ash from the tip, then slipped it carefully, frugally, into the pocket of his shirt.

There are seven hundred and fifty thousand people in the city of San Francisco and one or two of them took the trouble to look up as the black-and-white police helicopter came chattering over Union Square to land on the roof of the Hall of Justice. Harry Callahan was there to meet it, shuddering in the early morning wind. It was not raining, which was the only bright spot in what he felt sure would be a lousy day. Optimism had never been one of Harry's virtues at the best of times, and although he wasn't sunk in gloom, he wasn't exactly delirious with joy either. In the first place, his leg felt like hell. He was stiff from knee to crotch, and it was only through conscious effort that he was able to walk without yelping at each step. And in the second place, he had seen the morning edition of the *Chronicle* with the mayor's cryptic little note to Scorpio stuck away in the personal column. No one, outside of a tiny handful of people, would know what that message meant, but Scorpio would know and Scorpio wouldn't like it. Harry would gladly have bet a year's pay on that score.

TO SCORPIO: WE AGREE BUT NEED TIME TO GET MONEY. PLEASE BE PATIENT.

Harry swore under his breath. *Need time to get money.* If the killer had only half a brain, he'd realize that he was being conned. He'd smell the stall and it might just trigger something that would make Sandra Benson's death look like a love-in. No, Harry didn't like it and he showed his disapproval by spitting on the roof just as the helicopter touched down.

There was a two-man crew, young, sun-bronzed men who looked as though they didn't have a trouble in the world. They had been briefed but Harry went over it again—what to look for and what to do.

"A creep on a roof, could be anybody, male or female, skulking around with a rifle. We're after a psycho so take no chances. Observe and report. Have you got that? *Observe* and *report.* We don't give air medals for being gung ho, so don't be fancy. If you think the bastard will get away before we can handle it, then come in. But if you do anything, do it like you mean it. Don't try any target shooting, just hit him with a ten gauge."

The helicopter men exchanged solemn glances and went back to their machine. Harry stayed on the roof until the bird lifted off, banked sharply into the wind, and disappeared from view behind the soaring monoliths of the Golden Gateway Center.

Things were humming when he got back to the office. Di Georgio was setting pins in a wall map, three inspectors were on the phone, and Bressler was pacing back and forth inside his glassed-in cubicle like a chained leopard. When he saw Harry, he motioned him inside, and although his thigh was throbbing, Harry strolled into the office as casually as possible.

Bressler sat on the edge of his desk. "How's the leg feel?"

"Fine," Harry lied.

"Good. You're all luck, Harry. That was a nice bit of work yesterday. Even the commissioner called to extend his congratulations. Let me add my own. Did you see what they said about it in the paper?" Harry

31

looked blank. "They called it a classic example of how the police department protects the interests of the commonweal—whatever the hell *that* means. Anyway, congratulations." He smiled at Harry who did not respond at all. The lieutenant frowned. "I said . . . *congratulations.*"

"I heard you, Al."

"You could say thank you or something. It wouldn't kill you to be a little polite."

"I'd rather say thanks to a promotion and a raise in pay. Or isn't that in the interest of the commonweal?"

Bressler ignored the question. "Chicago police sent us a bulletin—something about a gun nut they're after. They think he might be in the bay area. Communications have all the details. I want you to check it out. It'll give you a chance to get acquainted with Gonsales."

"Who?"

"Charles Gonsales—your new partner." Bressler was looking everywhere but at Harry.

"I've got a partner," Harry said quietly. "Sam'll be back any day now."

"He'll be back, but not with you. He's being reassigned . . . city attorney's office . . liaison man."

"Liaison?" Harry spat out the word like phlegm.

"It's what he wanted and what his wife wanted. Sam's pushing forty and he's taken one bullet too many. He's not immortal, you know. I can't blame him."

Harry walked slowly over to a chair and sat down, stretching his bad leg in front of him. "Hell, I don't blame him either, but it's a kick in the ass. We've been partners for a long time."

"Nothing lasts forever." Bressler's tone was crisp, final. "Gonsales is a good man, young, on the ball. He'll learn fast."

Harry's face was a mask of bitterness. "You've got to be kidding, Al. I don't have the time to break in beginners. Why don't you give the kid a break and send him down to Bunko or Vice?"

"He stays here—with you."

"I'm tough on partners," Harry said darkly. "Fanduchi shot and killed . . . Sam with a hole in his lung. And then there was that kid, Joey what's-his-name, he—"

"Harry," Bressler cut in sharply, "you're working with Gonsales or you're not working. That's straight from the fifth floor so get used to the idea."

Harry slumped back in resignation. A new partner. It was a decided kick in the chest. A partner was more than just some guy to keep you company. A partner was an extension of your brain and hands. A partner had to think like you—act like you. It was deeper than a marriage. Charles Gonsales. Harry had never heard of him, which meant he was a rookie, a probationer. Jesus, he'd have to teach him everything . . . start from scratch . . . undo whatever the academy had taught him about solving a murder case . . . destroy his innocence and his illusions: *It's this way, Gonsales. Don't mess around too much looking for clues; a junkie whore with a big mouth will crack a case ten times faster than the crime lab*. So many facts of life that weren't in the book. A good cop kept his nose close to the street. He dealt with people he wouldn't spit on if he didn't need information. He tried to keep his hands clean, but any way you looked at it, it was a rotten business. How much of this would Charles Gonsales understand? How much of it would be repugnant?

"Harry, meet Gonsales." Bressler's voice cut across Harry's thoughts. He looked up and there was Charles Gonsales standing in the doorway. Harry wasn't overly impressed. Young, he thought, very young. A nice, clean-cut-looking Latin. Shine on his shoes . . . crease in his pants . . . new, well-cut sport coat . . . blue-striped shirt and wide tie. He looked like an insurance agent.

"Hi," Harry mumbled.

"Nice to meet you, Mr. Callahan. I've heard a lot about you." Gonsales took a step into the office with a smile on his face and his right hand extended in greeting. Harry just stared at it.

Gonsales hesitated a moment and then stuck his hand in his pocket. Sullen bastard, he thought. It was true that he had heard a good deal about Harry Callahan—but not much had been good.

Bressler smiled wryly. "One thing you'd better know about Harry, he's prejudiced. He doesn't like limeys, micks, hebes, dagos, pollacks, or American Indians. You name it and Harry hates it."

Gonsales forced a tight smile. "What about Mexicans?"

"Especially spiks," Harry replied blandly. He stood up, chewing the inside of his lip to keep from groaning. "Well, let's get on with it—partner. I'll teach you the drill. Anything you want to know, just ask."

"I'll do that, Mr. Callahan."

Harry ignored the sarcasm. There was part of him that liked it. He had a partner who wouldn't go around turning the other cheek. It would do for starters.

"You can stop calling me mister. Even my enemies call me Harry."

"OK," Gonsales said cautiously. "My friends call me Chico."

And that was that. They were partners, a team, for better or worse. Harry tried to size him up as they walked out of Bressler's office and down the hall to Communications. The kid walked well, not cocky, just free and easy. A man sure of his own body.

"What do you go?" Harry asked.

"One seventy-five," Chico said, his voice still bearing a note of cautious reserve. "I fought light heavy."

Getting better all the time, Harry mused. "How long did you fight?"

"Three years."

"I might have seen you around. Did you work any local clubs?"

Chico shook his head. "San Jose State."

34

Harry stopped in midstride and turned to face the younger man. "You might as well know it now, Chico. I don't like college boys."

"Maybe you just don't like me." Chico's eyes were like brown stones and they never left Harry's face.

"I don't know enough about you to have an opinion one way or the other, but I've never known a college boy yet who could go the distance in this department. Maybe it's the diploma; they think they're smarter than they really are. They do something stupid and some punk who never saw the fifth grade blows their head off with a shotgun. Don't let your diploma kill you— because I might get killed right alongside."

"I'll remember that." His voice was as hard as his eyes.

"OK," Harry snapped, "I've said my piece. Now let's get on with it. I've got a lot to fill you in on."

"There's just one thing I'd like to know," Chico said tightly. "Why do they call you Dirty Harry?"

Harry Francis Callahan did not reply. His lips had curled into a faint smile, but Chico Gonsales could see no humor in it.

"Like I was saying, I've got a lot to fill you in on." He strode off down the hall, a man going someplace and in a hurry to get there.

He had no name. No name at all. Maybe there had been a name once, but that had been a long time ago and the man had forgotten it. He had seen his name written on a piece of paper . . . his name had been typed so that it looked important, but he had known better. Beside the name there had been a date—also typed—in a little box marked Date of Birth. The date had been November 14, 1938. That had been important. That meant something. The day he was born. That was special. He was a Scorpio and Scorpios were special. He had read that in a book.

You are one who hits the world with dynamite in your personality. Dynamite and dynamics! That's your personality!

Yes! He was a Scorpio.

"I don't need any goddamn fuckin' name!" he shouted. No one could hear him. He was high on a building overlooking Washington Square; he stood looking down at the traffic snarled along Columbus Avenue, bumper to bumper, horns blowing.

"Pigs. Goddamn pigs."

He stood there for a long time, just staring down at all the cars, a sluggish metal river of cars, going nowhere. In his right hand he held the cheap brown suitcase and in his left, a newspaper.

There had been times, many years before, when he had tried to think about his name. He would remember it and then try to change it by turning all the letters around and rearranging them. No matter how he mixed the letters up the name still had meant nothing. But *Scorpio*. That was different. It had a ring to it. It meant something. He had kept it to himself. They would ask him his name. They would say: *Please tell us your name. Don't you know what your name is? Don't you want to tell us your name?*

"Bastards," he said into the wind. "Stupid bastards."

Why had they kept asking him what his name was? They knew what his name was. They had it typewritten on a piece of paper. They kept all the names in a file cabinet, hundreds of names, thousands of names. The names were clipped inside brown manila folders and the stupid bastards would have his name right on the desk in front of them while they asked him. Stupid bastards. Doctors, they said they were. Doctors! They weren't doctors, they were stupid bastards. Everyone knew that.

I don't have a name. Everyone has a name. Won't you tell us yours? Abcdefghijklmnopqrstuvwxyz. That's my name. My name is in there someplace but I lost it. You're so fuckin' smart, you find it.

36

And they would exchange glances and shake their heads.

"To hell with them."

He had always wanted to scream out SCORPIO! THAT'S MY NAME . . . SCORPIO. But Archie had said that if he did that they'd never let him go. He'd never get out of there if he did that. Scorpios were smart. They kept things to themselves. They were secret people. They had imagination—and a violent temper—*volcanic* the book said. He had been secret—and smart—and volcanic. He had snapped a nurse's neck to get out of there.

He squatted beside the rusty, creaking metal of a ventilator shaft, placing the suitcase carefully at his feet. He opened the newspaper and let the pages drift away one by one. He kept the first page of the classified section. He had circled one item in the Personal column with black crayon:

TO SCORPIO: WE AGREE BUT NEED TIME TO GET MONEY. PLEASE BE PATIENT.

"Please be patient. *Please* be *patient!*" His voice was a howl of mockery as he tore the page into tiny pieces. He flung the scraps into the air like confetti and watched them dance in the wind. "Oh, you bastards—you stupid bastards!"

He glared into space for a moment, his face dank with sweat, his eyes glassy with hate and anger. They were trying to make a fool of him. They were kidding him along. They had no right to do that. It had been a straight business deal. No complications. Simple. Why couldn't they see it that way? Why did they have to make it difficult for him by acting cute? *Please be patient.* A hundred thousand lousy bucks! The city made that in a day. They made more than that giving parking tickets! They could take that out of petty cash and never even miss it! *Please be patient.*

"Liars!"

His hands were trembling and he had difficulty in opening the suitcase. The rifle lay inside, each piece gleaming with a patina of oil. He assembled it with quick efficiency, snapped in a clip of shells, and carried the rifle to the edge of the roof.

"Beautiful," he whispered. He was crouched beside the iron framework of the fire escape, huddled in a tracery of shadow, difficult, if not impossible, to see from the street. The rifle barrel jutted out no more than a foot and he held it stationary on the only target he had in mind—the front doors of SS. Peter and Paul Roman Catholic Church.

"Here, priest," he intoned, "come on, priest. Step on out, priest. I'm waiting for you, priest. Come on."

But all that passed through the bright circle of the telescopic sight was an elderly woman going into the church with a white handkerchief pinned to the top of her hair.

Officer Miller pushed the stick over and eased his foot on the pedal. The helicopter responded to his feathery touch, swooping about and then hovering five hundred feet above Pier 45. Miller glanced at Officer Kilpatrick seated beside him with a board resting on his knees. On it was pinned a map of the city that gave the location of every rooftop in the North Beach and Russian Hill areas in which Tac Squad men were stationed.

"Where to now?" Miller shouted, his voice muted by the thump, thump, thump of the rotor blades.

"Swing over Coit Tower," Kilpatrick shouted back, "then Union to Van Ness."

"Rodger the Dodger," Miller yelled, grinning, playing wild blue yonder. "Wilco and out!"

Kilpatrick grinned back. He set the map board beside him and picked up his binoculars. Miller had eased forward on stick and throttle and the bird was moving now, chattering along at an even forty miles an hour over Fisherman's Wharf, across Jefferson, Beach, North Point, streets and buildings and rooftops gliding away beneath them. Kilpatrick swung the glasses slowly back and forth, but saw only tangles of TV antennas, clotheslines, a roofing crew swabbing hot tar, a plump girl in a sunsuit washing a small dog in a bucket.

"Any jaybirding going on today?" Miller asked.

Kilpatrick smiled to himself and shook his head. Sometimes, especially over the Hashbury, there would be naked couples on the roofs. Once they had seen a couple making love, the woman lying on an old mattress. She had looked up and waved.

Coit Tower stabbed at them, copper colored in the sun. Miller pivoted the chopper sharply and then leveled off, heading for the bright patch of Washington Square.

Kilpatrick spotted him almost by accident. He had seen nothing on the roof at first and was about to swing the glasses on ahead when he lingered for a moment to study a peculiar TV antenna. The aerial had more grids than the radar mast of a destroyer, and Officer Kilpatrick wondered idly what the hell it was used for. It was then that he spotted the suitcase and, a yard or two away from it, the crouched figure of a man.

"Hold it!" he yelped as the edge of the building slipped past and out of view. "Swing around again. There's a joker on the roof. I think he has a rifle."

Oh, God! Kilpatrick thought as Miller gunned the engine and swung the chopper about, what if it's him?

Just hit him with a ten gauge!

Inspector Callahan's unofficial instructions. Kilpatrick's hands felt damp as he reached for the shotgun standing in its bracket in front of him. He had never killed a man and he didn't relish starting now. Was it a rifle the man had been holding? He couldn't be sure. It could have been anything.

"There he goes," Miller called out. He was coming down toward the roof at a slight angle, rocking the chopper from side to side in order to keep the man in view. The man was confused, running in circles, staring up at the helicopter, his face white, mouth open, screaming.

Kilpatrick couldn't see clearly what the man was holding. Whatever it was, it was partially hidden behind the man's back. It could have been a rifle—then again it could have been a golf club.

Just hit him with a ten gauge! The shotgun would scatter the man all over the roof.

And what if it wasn't a rifle!

Kilpatrick grabbed the bullhorn instead and flicked it on. He leaned out the open side of the bubble canopy. "Stop! Stop in the name of the law! Stop or we'll shoot!"

The man didn't stop. He gathered up the suitcase and ran; he ran like a broken-field runner, like a frightened deer, through a tangle of aerial wires and down a stairwell.

"STOP! STOP!"

But the man was gone.

"How the hell could they let him get away?" Chico Gonsales asked bitterly.

Harry Callahan said nothing in reply. He sat hunched forward, both hands on the steering wheel, one eye on the slow-moving traffic ahead, the other on the crowded sidewalks of upper Grant Street.

"Had him cold," Chico went on. "I can't understand why they couldn't have come down very low—maybe not land, they might've wrecked the chopper—but just hover real low and then one of the guys could've jumped out and run after the suspect. Right? Or they could've just kept a close watch on the building . . . seen which way he came out. It seems to me—"

"Maybe they were talking so much they couldn't see anything," Harry said pointedly.

Chico thought that over. "It's possible."

"Clam up, then. Keep your eyes on the people."

A talker! If there was one quality that Harry couldn't stand in a partner, it was a loose mouth. Yakity-yakity-yakity. Chico Gonsales had said more words during the past six hours than Sam Fleming would have uttered in six months! Still, Harry had to admit that the kid was bright. He caught on fast, and he had an air of cool toughness. He wouldn't fold when and if things got rocky. Harry felt sure of that, and this made his big mouth a little easier to live with—but just a little.

They had been cruising the streets since the helicopter patrol had called in about the man on the roof. It was now early evening and it looked as if the guy had won the first round by getting away. That had been a bad break, but at least they had a good description, a description that kept coming over the radio every thirty minutes:

All units . . . be on the lookout for adult male Caucasian, last seen vicinity Washington Square. Suspect twenty-five to thirty-five, approximately five-ten, one hundred forty-five pounds, wearing tan chinos, yellow shirt, brown nylon windbreaker. May be carrying small brown suitcase, which could contain a thirty-thirty rifle. This man is wanted on suspicion of homicide and is to be considered extremely dangerous.

The call was not limited to the SFPD. It was being broadcast by the California Highway Patrol, and by the police departments in Oakland, Marin County, and down the peninsula as far south as Palo Alto and Mountain View. The killer could have been in Los Angeles by now, or over the Oregon line. Then again, he could be walking down Grant Street.

"Man in a brown windbreaker," Chico said quickly, tapping Harry on the shoulder with one hand and pointing with the other. Harry hit the brakes and looked off to his right. A man in tan pants and a brown windbreaker lounged against the side of a building picking his teeth with a matchstick.

Harry smiled. "That's Pistol Pete. Biggest pill pusher

41

in North Beach." He put his foot back on the gas pedal.

Chico frowned. "So? Why don't we pick him up? The description fits."

Harry chuckled softly. "Pete's a junkie. He couldn't hit a streetcar with a bucket full of peas. Besides, I wouldn't want to shake him up too much. He's a mine of information—an inexhaustible mine!"

"Police stooge," Chico said contemptuously.

"Don't knock 'em, Pancho."

"Chico," Chico said patiently for at least the tenth time that day. "I'm not knocking them, I just don't like them. You'd trust a fink like that?"

"Like he was my own mother."

"Why?"

"Because—Chico—he knows what I'd do to him if he told me a lie."

"Like railroad him to Quentin?"

Harry sighed deeply, as though the question was too sophomoric to answer. "No, of course not. I'd just take the man aside, talk to him, and then nail his tongue to a door."

Chico looked away, not altogether sure if Harry was kidding or not. He smiled wryly to himself. He had struggled to put himself through San Jose State—four years of work and study, study and work. But he had graduated top of his class with a bachelor's degree in sociology. *Sociology!* Harry Callahan should be easy to figure out—except that Harry Callahan didn't seem to fit into any known category of human behavior.

"Let's grab a bite," Harry said as he swung the car west on Filbert.

"Great, I know a nice little pla . . ." The word died in Chico's throat as he spotted a man dash across the street against the traffic—a man of medium height, dressed in tan pants and a windbreaker, carrying a suitcase in his right hand. A headlight beam held him for a fraction of a second and then he disappeared in the crowd. "Man with a suitcase!"

"Where?"

"Going up the street . . . north side . . . in the crowd."

Harry gunned the engine, but there was no going forward in a hurry. He was locked in—a truck in front, a taxi behind.

"Do you still see him?"

"No . . . *yes!* Turning into Medau Place."

Harry caught a quick glimpse of the man before he disappeared up the alley, walking quickly. A man of medium height . . . tan chinos . . . brown jacket . . . suitcase in his hand.

"Get out, Chico—block off Medau. It runs into Krausgrill, no other way out. I'll come in that way. Now *move.*"

Chico opened the door and half fell out of the car as Harry swung the wheel to the left and pulled out around the truck. He drove half a block on the wrong side of the street and then cut back in, forcing a car to give way, and parked in Krausgrill Place. The narrow alley went straight ahead for fifty yards and then turned sharply to the right. Harry ran to the corner, the magnum in his hand, and pressed his body against a wall. From somewhere down the alley he could hear the quick sound of footsteps—and then the banging of a door.

He bolted around the corner, the gun held in front of him. The alley stretched ahead, cluttered with trash cans and black as pitch. He moved into the darkness, one slow step after another, every nerve in his body as taut as stretched wire. There had been the sound of a door slamming, but that might have been a ruse. The man with the suitcase could be crouched behind a trash can with a rifle in his hands waiting for Harry to make just one mistake. Harry had no intention of doing so.

A light stabbed the darkness, streaming from the window of a three-story building halfway down the alley. Harry moved quickly toward it, dodging trash cans and packing crates, his body bent, moving like a soldier under fire. He knew the building. It was the back end of a run-down apartment house, a shooting gallery for addicts and a workhouse for whores. The light came from the bottom floor, but the window was too high for Harry to look into. Holstering his gun, he picked up a trash can, upended it, and set it carefully against the side of the building; then he climbed on top of it and peered around the edge of the window.

Tan chinos and brown jacket stood in the glare of a naked light bulb that dangled from the ceiling. His back was to Harry as he bent low over an unmade bed. The sheets were yellow with grime and they trailed on the floor as though whoever had slept between them had gotten up in a hurry. The man had placed his suitcase on the pillow and he was fumbling with the catches.

"Open it," Harry whispered harshly. He rested the barrel of the gun on the window ledge.

A door at one end of the room flew open and a woman emerged, a big, blowzy, pale-fleshed blonde.

"Jesus," Harry said in awe. She looked like the mother of every hooker in the world as she walked slowly toward the man, her great breasts rolling under a purple blouse, hips, belly, and buttocks bulging against the strained fabric of yellow satin slacks. The man turned toward her with a grin . . . a toothy Chinese smile.

The gun in Harry's hand began to waver. "Chinese?"

He slipped the magnum back in its holster, but he was rooted to the trash can by the tableau inside the room. The Chinese gentleman ogled the blonde for a moment, then turned quickly back to the suitcase, opened it, and dumped the contents on the bed. Wadded masses of dirty clothes tumbled out. The man fished through them and pulled out a small, neatly wrapped package, which he handed to the woman. She grabbed it eagerly, tearing the paper away while the man moved close to her, fondling her breasts, groping for the buttons on her slacks. He seemed to have four pairs of hands.

"Amazing," Harry whispered. It was like watching the opening scene of a pornographic film.

The woman undid the package and let the torn wrappings fall to the floor. She held up a minuscule nightgown, a baby doll, all frothy see-through nylon. It could only have been an erotic gesture on the man's part; the garment looked like a handkerchief in the woman's pudgy white hands. It wouldn't have fit her right arm let alone her entire body. She kissed him anyway, nibbling his ear while he tore and pulled at her slacks. Buttons popped and the slacks came down. Harry could see a flash of purple-veined thigh, a triangle of black lace panties, and then he was flying through the air.

It was fantastic. He had heard nothing . . . seen nothing . . . and now he was falling, clawing the air. He fell on his back and every ounce of wind left his lungs with a sound like an inner tube exploding. The trash can rolled past him, clanging away down the alley.

"Creep, goddamn motherin' creep!"

There were men all around him, big, ugly-looking guys. Harry saw them in multiple images. It looked like an army. He tried to focus his eyes and he tried to suck in enough air so that he could speak. He could do neither very well. "I'm a . . . puh . . . puh . . . leese . . ."

"You're a goddamn creep," one of the men snarled. "A lousy peeper."

"Call the cops," another said.

Harry staggered to his feet. "I am the co . . . p . . . s."

Someone hit him in the belly and he doubled over and went down on his knees.

"What did he say?"

"I think he said he was the cops."

"He's a freak. Look at him. A lousy pie-hawkin' pervert. Kick his chest in."

The men moved slowly, tightening the circle around

Harry, who lay like a fetus on the cold ground. Heavy motorcycle boots were being drawn back to kick him into oblivion when there was the sound of rapidly approaching footsteps.

"Hold it. All of you! Back against the wall!" Chico Gonsales moved toward the patch of light, a gun in his hand. The men hesitated and then drew back, eyeing the gun warily.

"Let 'em go, Chico," Harry gasped as he struggled to his feet.

"Let 'em go? They were assaulting a police officer."

"I said, let 'em go."

"He really is a cop," one of the men said in amazement. "How about that? We thought he was a freak."

"He *is* a freak," another one said. "He was standin' on that garbage can peekin' at Hot Mary and her boyfriend."

"Hot Mary?" Chico looked bewildered.

"Yeah, Hot Mary." A man jerked his head toward the lighted window. Chico looked and caught a glimpse of a naked woman, a mammoth display of white flesh, before a blind was drawn to shut off the view.

"All you guys," Harry said, grinding out the words, "get the hell out of here—move!"

They moved, drifting on up the alley like gray shadows.

"Hot Mary," Chico intoned. "How about that."

Harry brushed himself off and, with as much dignity as was possible, started walking back toward the car. Chico paced silently beside him until they reached it.

"I just had a thought."

"About what?" Harry growled.

"Why they call you Dirty Harry."

Harry mouthed a string of four-letter words and got into the car, slamming the door. The radio was crackling, repeating their code number. Harry reached over and flicked a switch.

"Inspectors seventy-one."

"About time." Sergeant Dixon's voice. "Got something for you, Harry. Potrero Hill—corner of Sierra and Texas. A young black boy."

"What about him?"

"Somebody shot him in the face."

IV

They took the James Lick Freeway and pulled off at Twenty-second Street, going flat out, the siren beneath the hood scattering the traffic. A flat sheet of white mist was drifting in from the bay and by the time they reached the corner of Sierra and Texas they were locked in.

There were black-and-white units all up and down Texas Street, their red lights revolving, bouncing off the mist, bathing everything in a scarlet glow. An ambulance stood in front of a vacant lot, its back doors open, the white-jacketed attendants standing in the street talking with some uniformed policemen. One of the policemen walked over to the blue Plymouth as Harry pulled up at the curb.

"Sergeant Reineke's up there in the grass, Mr. Callahan."

"The lab get here yet?"

The policeman shook his head soberly. "Not that I know of."

Harry got out of the car and looked down Texas Street. Shabby wooden frame buildings receded into the swirling mist. Doors were open and knots of people stood on front porches. Up the hill, beyond the vacant lot on Sierra, there was a line of four-story apartment houses and he could see flashlight beams moving back and forth across the roofs.

"Come on, Chico."

They walked through knee-high weeds to the center of the vacant lot. Several policemen and a tight, silent group of black men were standing around a blanket-covered bundle, from one corner of which protruded a small sneaker-clad foot.

"Who is he?" Harry asked quietly.

Sergeant Jim Reineke's tough, bulldog face was a hard mask. "His name was Charlie Russell. He was ten years old. One bullet—flush in the face." He paused for a moment and fixed Harry with a grim stare. "Get this guy, Harry."

Harry bent over and lifted a corner of the blanket. Chico stood beside him and saw, in the glare of a flashlight held by Sergeant Reineke, a sight that would sit on his mind for the rest of his life—a shattered, bloody clot of matter that had once been a little boy's face.

"Oh, Jesus Christ." He turned quickly to one side and vomited in the high grass.

Harry let the blanket fall and glanced at his retching partner, his mouth twisting into a sardonic grin.

"Welcome to Homicide, kid."

Chico looked up, his face sheened with sweat and the color of paste. He saw a look in Harry Callahan's eyes that belied the bitter wryness of his voice. He saw things in the man that he had not suspected were there —anguish, despair, compassion, and a deep, soul-burning pain.

Oh, you bastard, he thought wearily, Tommy Tough . . . all the way down the line . . . but a man's eyes never lied.

They stuck around for an hour. The lab men came and took pictures of Charlie Russell, late star pitcher of the Potrero Hill playground minor league, and the ambulance men took him away. It was all routine, professional—a job. They could have been carting away a dead cat. Harry and Chico just stood around, waiting for Reineke's Tactical Squad team to come down from the roofs. When they did, one of them had a thirty-thirty shell casing in a small plastic bag.

"That seals it," Reineke said. "It's your boy, all right. But a kid . . . why would he pick a little kid?"

"He was black, wasn't he?" Harry plucked the shell casing out of the sergeant's hands and walked to the car.

Two brass shell casings left on rooftops, one crazy note, a description of a man that could fit half the men in northern California. It all added up to zero.

"Someone must have seen him," Harry said. He sat in the car and stared gloomily down Texas Street. The streetlights were dim halos glowing in the mist.

"Not in this soup," Chico said quietly. He felt drained and of no use to anyone.

Harry glanced at him. "There probably wasn't any fog when he got here. Hell, a white cat carrying a suitcase might just have been spotted."

"Maybe." Chico's voice was listless.

Harry eyed him with concern. "You aren't the first guy to chuck up his guts. It doesn't make you a bad cop, you know . . . just proves you're human."

Chico forced a smile. His face was pale and his eyes were still watery. "Thanks, Callahan."

Harry snorted and switched on the engine. "Don't start getting formal on me, *Pancho*. The name's still Harry."

They drove slowly through the mean, fog-shrouded streets of Potrero Hill. Black faces stared at them, mute, impassive.

You see a white guy . . . medium height . . . about thirty years old? Might have been wearing tan chinos and an old brown windbreaker . . . maybe carrying a suitcase?

No, sir. Didn't see no one. No, sir, not me.

"There are some people around here who wouldn't tell their mother the right time," Harry said bitterly. He turned down a narrow alley and drove through wreaths of almost impenetrable fog into Mississippi Street.

Chico was impressed. "You sure know your way around."

"I was born here. I'm a Potrero Hill boy." He glanced out the side window, at the ramshackle wooden buildings with their blistered Victorian facades. "Some things never change in this life and the hill is one of them."

You see a man . . . medium height . . . tan chinos . . . brown windbreaker?

Not me, I didn't see nobody.

"They grow up not trusting the cops," Harry said bitterly. "They learn it before they can walk. We had beat cops when I was a kid. When I was six years old, I threw a brick at one of them. He picked it up and threw it right back. They didn't teach cops sociology in those days. I don't know, maybe we were all better off. I just don't know."

See a man come by here about seven . . . eight o'clock? Tan chino pants . . . brown suitcase?

Saw two men carryin' a piano but they wasn' either of 'em wearin' chinos. One of 'em was wearin' a suit . . . a ol' blue suit.

"Comedians. If you don't have a sense of humor, you'll crack like glass. There are more comics on Potrero Hill than any place on earth."

Seven tall, gangly boys lounged around a lamppost, flicking a basketball from one to the other. Harry pulled over and Chico leaned out the window.

"Hi, fellas. Mind if I ask you a couple of questions?"

"Go ahead," one of the boys said, "if you'll let me ask you one first. See, I got me a friend . . . an', well, he say it's true an' I say it ain't."

"What?" Chico asked, smiling, friendly and reachable.

"That pigs eat shit!"

The boys scattered, screaming with derisive laughter, whirling away into the fog.

Chico rolled up his window. *"They* were hilarious. Just a laugh a second."

Harry sat slumped behind the wheel, his long fingers drumming a slow tattoo on the rim. "We'll never get the guy this way, Chico. Never in a million years. This isn't a crime lab and legwork kind of case. Hell, he told us what he was going to do and he went right ahead and did it. *Kill a priest,* he said ... *kill a nigger.* Well, that roof the chopper boys scared him off of faces a Catholic church. He didn't get his priest so he butchered Charlie Russell instead. He won't let it go at that, Chico. He promised us a dead priest and he'll deliver one."

Chico whistled softly through his teeth. "There are a lot of churches and a lot of priests in this city, Harry. We can't watch all of them."

"That's right. But we only have to watch *one.*" Harry floored the gas pedal, made a sharp U-turn, and headed toward the freeway.

"Where are we going?"

"Back to the barn. Make sure you get a good night's sleep because I have a feeling tomorrow is going to be one hell of a day."

The chief of police had a smooth, round face and a shock of snow white hair. His eyes were pale blue, clear and kindly. He was nicknamed the Bishop, a sobriquet that reflected the respect everyone in the department held for him. He had been a policeman for a long, long time and had seen many changes in the city and in the nature of its crimes. He was by nature a thinking law officer who abhorred violence.

The word is enforcement, not force, was one of his pet sayings. However, he had learned how to use force when circumstances pressed him to do so. He was being pressed now; but although it might be necessary, he didn't have to like it. He eyed the heavy gun case in Lieutenant Bressler's hands with trepidation.

"You're fighting fire with fire, Al, and I'm not sure that I go for it. What kind of rifle is that anyhow?"

"A four fifty-eight Winchester."

The chief stirred uncomfortably in his chair. "You could kill an elephant with a gun like that. Apparently you like a little edge."

"All we can get," Harry said. He walked over and stood beside Bressler, taking the rifle case from him and placing it on the chief's desk. "A four fifty-eight will stop him even if I just hit him on the finger. A ten-power scope goes with it. It's a big package."

"Yes," the chief intoned, "a big package."

He leaned back and eyed the three men standing before him. They were sweating, which didn't surprise him. It was warm in his office with the midmorning sun beating on the windows. The chief had a bronchial condition that made air conditioning a torment rather than a luxury. The cooling vents in the walls had been sealed over and the air in the room was humid, like the interior of a greenhouse.

"I wish we could do it without all the artillery. A stakeout—and a grab."

Harry shook his head. "No way. This guy's a crack shot. He'd drill somebody between the eyes before we got within ten feet of him."

"I suppose you're right. Do you have any doubts about this, Al?"

"No," Bressler said. "All the pieces fit. It could work."

"It will work," Harry said fiercely. "We'll be looking right down his throat."

Chico frowned slightly and the chief noticed his expression.

"Anything bothering you, inspector?"

"No," he said quickly, "nothing."

"Speak out, Gonsales," Harry said dryly, "you're among friends."

"Well, it seems like such a . . . a long shot. I mean, why would he come back to the same roof?"

The chief reached into a large humidor on the desk

and drew out a cigar. He left the lid open as a gesture of courtesy but nobody made a move to take one.

"That's a pretty fair question, Harry. Seems like a hell of a long shot to me, too—maybe two thousand to one."

Harry shook his head sharply. "No, chief. Let me run through it again and you'll see how the odds change. I admit we're playing a long shot and the whole thing could pull up lame, but I know what kind of a person we're after. The guy's psychotic and, at the moment, frustrated. We stopped him from doing the first thing he promised he'd do—kill a priest. There's no doubt in my mind he was up on that building so he could draw a bead on SS. Peter and Paul's front doors. When the chopper came in, he ran away. That night he killed a black—the other part of his promise, but I'll bet my badge it angered him. I've dealt with psychotics and sociopaths all my life. They love patterns and routines. They hate anything to go wrong or out of sequence. I've known them to rob the same store six . . . seven times in a row. I've seen them try to pull a holdup when there were cops crawling all over the place simply because they had planned to pull the job that day. They don't give a damn. It makes them feel audacious. Like the Scarlet Pimpernel or Black Bart. Scorpio strikes again!! They like that feeling."

The chief mulled it over. "The odds go down—a bit."

"They go down more than a bit," Harry went on. "They're having a novena tonight at Peter and Paul's."

"There are still a lot of other buildings on the square he could use," the chief interjected dubiously.

"Sure there are," Harry admitted, "and every key one will have a couple of our men on it before sundown. We're going for high visibility. Let him see 'em up there walking around. The only roof that won't be covered is the one he was on yesterday. He'll go for it like a homing pigeon and Gonsales and I will be on the building in back of it—two stories higher up—breathing on his neck. How do you figure the odds now, chief?"

The chief pursed his lips and passed the cigar under his nose. "It's worth a two-dollar bet, Harry, any day in the week. Did you get the extra helicopters you wanted?"

Lieutenant Bressler, feeling a little left out of it, was quick to answer. "They're up there now: Fire Department, Harbor Division, and one from Contra Costa. All those choppers wheeling around'll keep him off the roofs during daylight."

"Good." The chief looked pleased. "Very good."

Bressler rewarded himself by snagging a cigar from the humidor and tucking it into his breast pocket. "That about covers the operation, chief. It's pretty much up to Harry and Gonsales now."

"In that case," the chief remarked drolly, "you might've grabbed a cigar for them, too."

The stakeout is the most delicate of all police procedures. The more men involved in it, the better the chance for it to go wrong. The Washington Square stakeout had to be big and it had to be complex. No one knew better than Harry Callahan just how delicate the whole thing was. If the killer sensed the presence of the police, he would stay clear, and yet the police had to be handy in order to seal off the building should he enter it. Harry conceived the operation to work in two phases—the lead-on and the trap. The lead-on men were the uniformed patrolmen on the rooftops. They were the bait that would draw the killer to the only unprotected building on the square. If the killer had been normal, such an obvious lure would have scared him off, but he was not normal.

"He's a nut," Harry said flatly, "but like all psychos he thinks he's smarter than anybody else. When he sees that building, he'll just know he's smarter than we are. Good. I want him to think that. I want that bastard to crow."

Five teams of inspectors, ten men in all not including Harry and Chico, sat in the briefing room of the Union Street police station nine blocks from Washington Square. The time was four thirty in the afternoon—two and one-half hours before sunset.

Inspector Di Georgio pursed his lips in thought and made some doodles on his note pad. "What if he smells detective before he goes into the place, Harry?"

"He won't smell anybody, Frank. Any team that comes within two blocks of the building before getting the word from me gets chopped off at the ankles. Stay clear of Columbus, Powell, Stockton, and any other street leading directly to the square."

"What about Price Lane for me and Kirby?" Joe Weston asked.

Harry nodded. "Price Lane is fine. Any of those alleys off Union will do as long as you can read me on the walkie-talkie. Any more questions?"

The men shook their heads soberly and started to rise.

"Just one more thing," Harry cautioned. "Be extra careful if you do come in. This guy's handy with a gun and he doesn't have a damn thing to lose!"

They struggled up a narrow staircase toward the roof, Harry in front carrying the big Winchester in its case, a walkie-talkie, and a pair of binoculars. Chico brought up the rear, cursing softly, a big portable spotlight in his hands, a battery case dangling from one shoulder. The equipment may have been portable but it was heavy as lead and the darkness of the stairs was of no help at all.

"You'd think they'd have a goddamn light up here!" he said savagely.

"Take it up with the super." Harry came in contact with the door to the roof and banged it open with his shoulder. He stepped out into a riot of flashing colors. Towering thirty feet above the roof was a metal sign, as broad as a billboard, turning creakily around and

56

around, proclaiming to all of North Beach in pink-and-green neon that

JESUS SAVES   JESUS SAVES   JESUS SAVES

Harry stared up in awe. "That enough light for you, Chico?"

Chico gazed at it, his face turning from pink to green and back to pink. "It's a comfort."

"It's a problem, but we'll have to live with it. That light's been on every night for the past twenty years. Our boy might have smelled a rat if it went off tonight. Keep low and follow me." He led Chico at a crouch across the roof to the low coping around the edge. A black chasm yawned below them. Harry sat with his back to the coping and rested the rifle beside him. Chico remained standing, eyeing the roof of the other building across the alley. It was deserted. Or was it? Tin ventilator housings dotted it, casting black wedges of shadows. A dozen men could have been hidden there. Harry glanced at him and shook his head in wonder.

"With that light behind you, Chico, you're about as hard to spot as Coit Tower. I said low and I mean *low!*"

Chico dropped to one knee beside the coping and put the lamp and the battery case behind him. "Where do you want me to set up this thing?"

"About ten yards to my right."

Chico nodded slowly, a worried expression tugging the corner of his mouth. "Guess you know this light's going to draw his fire, don't you?"

Harry mulled it over for a second. "Maybe you'd better make that *fifteen* yards."

Surveillance is simply another word for waiting—usually in a dark and lonely place. Harry Callahan and Chico Gonsales waited on a rooftop, bathed in a cold glare of neon, shivering in a brisk fog-laden wind. Far

below them people moved through Washington Square
—hippies with guitars, coveys of girls in miniskirts or
hot pants, squadrons of sailors hoping to pick one up,
old men slumped on benches reading newspapers in the
glow of lamplights, and a few people strolling toward
the open doors of SS. Peter and Paul.

Harry took it all in, moving his binoculars slowly
from one passing scene to the next.

"Anything?" Chico called out softly.

Harry put down the glasses and picked up the walkie-
talkie. "Not a damn thing," he replied wearily, pressing
the button. "Inspectors seventy-one . . . inspectors seventy-one. Who reads me? Over."

The voice of Frank Di Georgio crackled in his ear.
"How's the weather up there? Over."

"It stinks. Everything stinks. No sign—nothing. We'll
give it another hour. Over and out."

He slumped back in disgust, placing the instrument
beside him and taking up the binoculars again. The
scene had not changed much. A few less couples. One
of the old men had placed his newspaper over his face
and was lying stretched out on the bench. A priest
stood in front of the church, walking slowly back and
forth as though in meditation.

Chico crawled over to him. "Who's that dressed up
like a padre?"

Harry lowered the glass for a second. "Father Anthony Columbo—in his own suit."

Chico sucked in his breath. "Does he know we're
using him for bait?"

"Father Anthony Columbo had three years with the
82nd Airborne before he put his collar on backward.
When I warned him that somebody might take a pot-
shot at him he just laughed in my face."

"Well," Chico said, "like the sign says, Jesus saves."

The minutes slipped by and the wind changed from
cold to frigid. Streamers of gray mist drifted out of the

darkness and were turned into pink and green plumes by the neon. Harry swept the area with tired eyes. The church was closing—the last few worshipers leaving, nodding to Father Columbo before scurrying off into the deepening fog. It was then that he saw it, a vague movement out of the corner of one eye, a mere change in the shape of a shadow. Somebody was on the other roof.

Harry dropped flat below the coping and pressed the walkie-talkie button. "Inspectors seventy-one . . . inspectors seventy-one. Fish are biting . . . fish are biting."

"What is it?" Chico whispered harshly.

"The son of a bitch took the bait." He handed over the glasses. "Right corner . . . next to the ventilator."

Chico's hands were trembling slightly from cold, anticipation, and a healthy dose of fear. He adjusted the focus and the roof—fifty feet away and three stories below—jumped sharply at him. A man squatted by the ventilator, peering around it at Washington Square.

"Get back to your light," Harry snapped. "When I sing out, hit him with it. He'll jump like a rabbit so try not to lose him."

"Right!" Chico crawled quickly back to his position.

Harry picked up the Winchester and rammed home a big four fifty-eight cartridge, the shell popping up noiselessly from the magazine and sliding into the chamber. The safety stuck and he cursed it, softly but vehemently, until the lever gave way with a loud click.

Had the man heard the sound? It didn't seem possible, and yet Harry could sense the tenseness of the shadowy figure as he picked him up in the scope. The man had stiffened, half crouching, like a wild animal sniffing the wind for danger.

"He's going to bolt!" Harry thought. He held the dark form steady in the cross hairs and shouted, "Now!"

The flood lamp snapped on, the hot white light searing the mist. The beam missed the man by a good two feet, striking the edge of the ventilator and cutting a path of noon across one section of the roof.

BLAM

Harry fired to the left of the light path and saw a piece of the ventilator spin off into the darkness.

"Left!" he shouted. "Left!"

Chico shifted the lamp, easily, not jerking it, the beam catching the legs of the killer as he raced across the roof toward a stairwell, zigzagging through a maze of clotheslines.

BLAM

The elephant slug howled as it ricocheted off the roof at the man's feet, slicing a ten-foot groove in the tar paper. The man twisted his body in midstride and fired from the hip, a snap shot aimed at the light. The bullet hit the edge of the coping midway between Harry and the lamp. Chunks of brick and mortar whistled through the air like shrapnel.

BLAM

A clothesline pole snapped, the broken end whirling into the air, trailing a line of laundry behind it like the tail of a kite.

"Goddamn it!" Harry exploded.

The killer dove for the safety of the elevator housing, flattening himself against the side. Harry could see the barrel of the man's rifle projecting around it, and he aimed carefully for the corner of the stucco wall.

BLAM

The corner dissolved in dust and flying fragments and the killer moved out, bent over, firing from the hip, the muzzle flashes long tongues of flame spurting from the silencer. A bullet hummed past Harry's head like a savage bee and another tore the lamp from Chico's hands, spraying him with powdered glass.

"You OK, Chico?" Harry called out.

Chico sat back, staring numbly at the ruined lamp. "I . . . I think so . . . yeah."

Harry cursed the darkness. He could see nothing on the opposite roof but tangled shadows, which he traversed slowly, praying for one of the shadows to move.

"Come on, you bastard," he whispered, "make a run for it."

He did, but he ran firing, the gun coughing harshly, spitting flame, the bullets blasting into the revolving sign. Neon tubing popped and fell. Electric wires whipped downward trailing flashing blue sparks. A severed metal grid plunged seven stories to the street, dashing a pink JESUS into oblivion.

"We missed him!" Harry's voice was a howl of bitterness. He had seen nothing but the smooth flicker of the muzzle flashes as the man had raced for the stairwell. Before he could return the fire, the man had gone.

"Let's go!" Harry held the rifle in both hands and dashed for the door, plunging into darkness, taking three steps at a time in his wild charge down the stairs. He came out the rear of the building into the alleyway, Chico right behind him with his revolver drawn and cocked.

Nothing moved, but the night was electric with the scream of sirens as patrol cars converged on the building from all directions. Harry pointed up the alley. "Cover the front, Chico!" As Chico ran toward the brightly lit street, Harry moved deeper into the dark canyon between the two buildings, the rifle pressed against his hip, finger taut on the trigger. He walked slowly, one cautious step at a time, eyes probing every shadowed doorway, every pile of trash. He turned the corner of the building and went down another alley, narrower, darker, more sinister than the one he had left. His hands were clammy and the big rifle felt unwieldy

61

in such a narrow space. He knew that if anything happened it would happen with whirlwind speed and he was debating with himself whether or not to lay the rifle down and continue the search with his handgun when he slipped on something and stumbled, falling hard to one knee. A short, harsh, four-letter word jerked from his lips as he regained his footing. His left wrist hurt from bracing his fall and he could feel the cold night air on his right kneecap where the asphalt had ripped a hole in his pants. He felt something else, too—something wet and sticky on his fingers. It had the feel of oil . . . or blood.

"What the hell." Harry looked down. A small, black puddle lay at his feet, fed by a rivulet that wormed across the alley from a dark pile of ash cans stacked against the side of the building. Something was lying against them like a bundle of old clothes. As he walked toward it, Inspector Di Georgio and three officers came barreling around the corner of the building, shotguns and flashlights in their hands.

"Over here!" Harry yelled. "Need some light."

The flashlights bounced crazy patterns down the alley as the men ran toward him. A beam wavered, then held, turning the thin black stream into a ribbon of crimson . . . turning the bundle of old clothes into the sprawled, bloody form of Inspector Joe Weston.

Frank Di Georgio placed his shotgun on the ground and knelt beside the body. The others stood beside him, their flashlight beams forming a circle of light about the two men. Di Georgio made his examination quickly, going by the book, doing what he was trained to do even though he had known on first seeing Joe Weston that there would be no flicker of life, no response to the pressure of his fingertips on Joe's wrist. He glanced up at the silent figure of Harry Callahan.

"He's dead. One shot . . . in the chest."

Harry nodded. His mouth was full of dry ashes and the Winchester felt heavy and useless in his hand.

"He must have run right into the bastard," Di Georgio said quietly. "He hadn't even drawn his gun yet. You warned him about that, Harry. You told him the guy was dangerous."

"I missed the son of a bitch, Frank." Harry's voice was toneless. "You could stop an elephant with a gun like this and I missed him."

Di Georgio looked away from Harry and got slowly to his feet. "So, you missed him." He bent over and retrieved his shotgun. "Joe shouldn't have come down here without a gun in his hand. You warned him, Harry."

"Sure." Harry turned sharply and walked back the way he had come, toward the lights of Washington Square and the howling sirens.

A big package. A complex operation designed to trap a man on a rooftop. But nothing had come but a shadow—and death.

*I come and they are drawn to me by the power of
my personality. The man who went to the moon is a
Scorpio . . . the vice-president is a Scorpio. Scorpios do
great things . . . they attract people. They are magnetic.*

"You're pretty," the man said. "You're a very pretty
girl."

The girl giggled and squirmed on the seat beside him.
"Oh, wow."

"I saw you come out of the movie and walk to the
bus stop. I said to myself . . . that's a very pretty
girl—pretty and nice."

"You talk funny. You know that? Kinda *nice* . . .
but funny."

"I'm a nice person. I'm a Scorpio."

"Oh, wow, astrology." She giggled again and moved
her head, tossing her long, straight hair.

He glanced sideways at the girl while he drove. He
could only see her clearly when he passed the street-
lamps. Her image seemed to flicker like an old silent
film, but she was young, very young, with a smooth
oval face framed with blond hair. She wore a baggy
red sweater and a short skirt that rode far up on plump,
white thighs.

Want a lift?

Where are you going?
Anywhere . . . just driving around.
Will you take me to Portola and Sloat?
Sure, hop in.
Oh, wow, that's groovy.
Are you hungry?
Oh, wow.
How about a nice hamburger and a malt?
Oh, wow.
Or a pizza and a Coke.

He reached over and placed his right hand on the inner part of her left thigh, his fingers digging into the firm, cool flesh. She stiffened and looked at him, her eyes wide, startled.

"Tell me," he asked softly, "have you ever seen the face of God?"

The sea is cold and it moves under the cold stones. The water moves under the rocks and the rocks are black. If I throw a stone into the air, it will fall through the darkness to the bottom of the sea.

The man tossed a stone from the heights but he could not see it fall. He strained his ears and heard a dull plop as the stone hit the water.

"Down to the bottom of the sea," he said.

He sat hunched in the darkness, hands clasping his thin knees, rocking slowly back and forth on his heels. It was windy and cold on the promontory but his body felt hot and clammy. It would be dawn in an hour. He could tell that by looking at the stars. He knew a great deal about the stars and their paths through the heavens. He knew where every star should be at a certain time of night and at a certain time of the year. The stars were constant. They never disappointed him. He knew their names by heart and could repeat them like a litany.

Antares . . . Sirius . . . Vega . . . Spica . . .

The stars were his friends. Especially Antares and the other stars of Scorpio. He looked toward the sky but the towering base of the Golden Gate Bridge blocked off a good part of the star patterns. A car went over the bridge, the sound of its passage loud in the stillness of the night.

"Bastards," the man said. "Rotten bastards."

The anger was returning, cutting into him with a sharp, hot ache. He began to sweat more freely and his breath was labored.

"Fuckin' bastards!"

The wind tore his words to shreds. He stood up, trembling, and walked back up the steep, narrow path to where he had left his car. It would be dawn soon and he still had many things to do.

It was a rotten morning, gray and dank, the fog sliding over the city like a dirty sheet. Harry Callahan eyed it through the dingy glass of an all-night eatery on Filbert Street. He didn't like what he saw, but then he wouldn't have been ecstatic over a bright spring day either the way he was feeling. He sipped his coffee and stared moodily through the window at the deserted street.

"It was just a lousy break," Chico Gonsales said. He had repeated that observation over a dozen times and the phrase still had no meaning—least of all to Harry.

"I had the son of a bitch cold," he muttered. He took another sip of coffee. He wasn't eating his heart out about it, but it rankled. He should have blown the killer in half with the Winchester, but then Joe Weston should have known better than to run down a dark alley without his partner backing him up. He should have had his gun out. He had made a mistake and now he was dead. They would engrave his name on a small golden star and affix it to the police memorial plaque in the lobby of the Hall of Justice. There were a lot of names on that plaque and now Joe Weston's would be one of them.

"Where do we go from here?" Chico's voice was weary.

Harry shrugged and drained his coffee. "Back over the same ground."

Chico looked dubious. "It's a cold trail, Harry."

"Maybe . . . maybe not."

It was cold and Harry knew it. And yet . . . somebody could have seen something . . . anything. The killer had come to the building and then left it. How had he come? By bus? Taxi? Car? If by car, where had he parked it? On the street? Parking lot? Down an alley? They had spent all night checking it out, talking to a score of people who had been in or around Washington Square during the time of the shoot-out. All of them had heard the shots but no one had seen anything.

A man carrying a suitcase? Tan chino pants? Light brown windbreaker? No . . . no . . . can't say that I saw anybody like that.

A pale man. A shadow man. A blender. Just one of the crowd. Faceless. Nondescript. A hundred people might have seen him, but why bother to remember it? A person could see a thousand other people in a day and not be able to recall one of them. Why should they? There was no reason on earth why anyone would notice this man. And yet—

"We'll keep beating the bushes. Here . . . Russian Hill and Potrero. Something might jibe. This character gets around, Chico. It's my hunch he drives a car. We'll work that angle. It's slim, God knows, but sometimes people will remember a car and not the driver. You know, a bashed-in fender—an old model—something that sticks in the mind. If we could just tie a car into two of the killings, we might have a little thing going for us."

Chico looked even more dubious than he had before. "Talk about long shots."

Harry ignored the pessimism. "We'll start at the Russell killing. Those Potrero Hill kids have an eye for cars. We'll fan out from Sierra and Texas and see what we come up with. In the meantime, Di Georgio and Baker can work Washington Square while Silvero and

Marcus cover the Carlton Tower area. Then we'll compare notes. If any two descriptions match, we have us a lead." He glanced away from Chico's expressive eyebrows. He was clutching for the slimmest of straws. He knew it, and he knew Chico knew he knew it. He uttered a great monument of a sigh and stood up, fishing in his pocket for small change. Chico beat him to it, tossing some silver on the counter top.

"This might be a foolish question, *amigo,* but when do we get some sleep?"

"Why?" Harry growled. "Are you tired?"

They prowled the streets east of the General Hospital, the state name streets of Potrero Hill—Texas and Carolina, Wisconsin and Arkansas, Mississippi and Pennsylvania. Fawn-eyed black youths paused in their games and answered questions, warily at first, then more eagerly as their interest was aroused.

A car, man? What car? I ain't got no car. I'm a skate board fiend. I travel ca-leen. None of that lead-in-the-air jazz for me, man.

Saw a blue Chevy . . .

A black Ford . . . Torino . . . real class.

Jaguar.

'56 Merc . . .

Edsel! Swear to God!

Red Pinto with mag wheels . . .

"It's a bummer," Chico said. It was ten thirty-five in the morning, and a dull orange sun was starting to burn off the fog in patches. The sky was a blanket dotted with moth holes.

"Let's hit Twenty-second Street again and then check in with Di Georgio and—"

The radio crackled and the voice of the operator cut across Harry's words. "Inspectors seventy-one . . . inspectors seventy-one."

Chico reached forward and flicked the switch. "Inspectors seventy-one."

"Inspectors seventy-one. Report to Lieutenant Bressler's office. Code two."

"On our way," Chico said. He looked at Harry. "What's up?"

Harry set his jaw and pressed the accelerator to the floorboards. He burned rubber, to the screaming delight of the street kids, and headed up Twenty-third Street toward the freeway with the siren wailing. When Bressler called a code two, he meant a code two.

There was an air of tension in the inspectors' room as Harry and Chico came into it. Harry could sense it immediately. It was reflected in the drawn face of Frank Di Georgio and the pacing figure of Lieutenant Bressler seen through the glass door. Harry went straight into his office.

"Well?"

Bressler needed a shave and his eyes were sunken. He looked at Harry for a long moment before speaking. Then:

"It's a whole new ball game, Harry. He grabbed a fourteen-year-old girl."

"When?"

"Some time last night. Her name's Mary Ann Deacon. She went to the movies and never came home. Her parents weren't too worried when she didn't get back by midnight. She's a big, mature girl with a raft of boyfriends. They thought she might have met one of them and gone on a little necking session—or whatever the hell big, mature girls do these days. By three in the morning, they phoned the police and Juvenile were out looking for her. They needn't have bothered." He turned sharply away from Harry and picked up a shoe box from his desk. It had been wrapped in plain brown paper, part of which had been torn off.

"It was addressed to the mayor. The bomb squad looked it over first, then sent it to us . . . as soon as they found *this* inside." He opened the lid and took out

a folded piece of paper, which he handed to Harry.
"Read it."

It was a note, written with a soft lead pencil, each
letter perfectly formed as though traced from a child's
book on penmanship. Harry read aloud for the benefit
of Chico who stood in the doorway behind him.

" 'Mary Ann Deacon. Buried alive.' " A sliver of ice
became wedged in his spine. He could hear Chico's
sharp intake of breath and the thumping of his own
heart.

"Buried alive?"

"Keep on reading," Bressler said, his voice hushed.

Harry looked back at the painfully neat script.
" 'Double-crossing police bastards made me do this.
It's on your pig heads. Ransom for this bitch two hundred thousand dollars in used tens and twenties. One
man with suitcase. Marina at Divisidaro. 9 P.M. She
has oxygen till 3 A.M. tomorrow. Red bra and panties.
Big tits. Mole on left thigh.' The son of a bitch!"

"No comments, Harry . . . just read."

Harry gripped the paper so tightly his knuckles turned
white with the strain. He read on, speaking with difficulty, his voice tight as a wire.

" 'All OK you get location of girl by 2 A.M. Pull
anything cute and the girl dies. Slow suffocation.
Signed . . . Scorpio.' " He held out the paper to Bressler
with two fingers. "Fumigate it."

Bressler took it, folded it carefully, and slipped it
into a manila envelope. "There were no prints. He's a
very careful man, this Scorpio. Very careful and very
thorough. He doesn't kid around. Take a look in the
box."

Harry stepped over to the desk and dumped the
contents of the box on the smooth, uncluttered surface.
There was a red brassiere, 36 B cup; a pair of red nylon
panties; a lock of blond hair tied into a tight knot; and
a molar, the roots caked with dried, black blood.

"Her dentist identified the tooth," Bressler said quietly. "He said it was yanked out with a coarse instrument—like a pair of pliers."

"She's dead," Harry said. "You know that, don't you, Al?"

"All I know is what the note says. She'll be alive till 3 A.M."

"She's dead." He put the articles back into the box, carefully, one item at a time.

Bressler faced him, flushed and angry. "We're not going to second guess this guy, Harry. We're going to do *exactly* what he tells us . . . right down the line . . . no tricks. We had our play last night and all we have to show for it is a good man dead and Mary Ann Deacon. The mayor's raising the money on his own . . . private funds . . . individual contributions. He's using up a lot of favors, Harry. He's going to pay off. All he wants is a bagman."

It was suddenly very quiet in the office, only the gentle whir of the air-conditioning system in the wall breaking the silence. Bressler's face was a taut mask and Harry stared straight into it.

"That's a crap job."

Bressler nodded. "He could get the bagman in a dark place, blow his head off, and take the money. You're right, it's a crap job. Do you want it?"

Harry looked down at the open box, at the bloody tooth, the red panties neatly folded. "Sure . . . what the hell."

"Good," Bressler said crisply. "Be in the chief's office at 6 P.M.—sharp!"

Chico had stood by silently, but as Harry started toward the door and Lieutenant Bressler turned back to his desk he felt compelled to say something.

"Where do I fit in?"

Bressler answered without looking at him. "You don't. You're out of it."

Chico Gonsales came from a long line of hot-blooded, quick-tempered people. He had a low boiling point and his summary dismissal in no way raised it.

71

"I don't buy that."

Bressler stiffened as though slapped in the face. "What did you say, Gonsales?"

"I said, I don't buy it. No cover . . . one man . . . are you sure that's the way to do it?"

"No." Bressler's voice was frigid. "I'm not sure, but that's the way we're doing it."

"You're going to get a good man killed."

The lieutenant's face was the color of port wine. He pointed a finger at Gonsales, a finger that quivered. "Now you just wait a minute, Gonsales."

"No, I won't wait a minute. I may be new here but I'm not stupid. I know why they call him Dirty Harry . . . yes, I know now. Every rotten, cruddy job that comes along, he gets it—the dirty end of the stick! Harry was right. It's a crap job and you've got no business . . . no *right* to send him on it alone."

"You just keep talking, Gonsales, and I'll bounce you right out of here! I'll have you walking a beat on a goddamn pier!"

Bressler reached for a phone but Harry placed a hand on his wrist. "Take it easy, Al. He's had a bad couple of days. Why not split the difference? Give him the night off instead."

Bressler moved his big head like a dog shaking water out of its ears. "Get the hell out of here—both of you."

Harry grinned and left, taking Chico with him, a hand firmly on the younger man's arm. They walked over to Harry's desk in the far corner of the inspectors' room.

"What were you playing? Pancho Villa? You go gunning for the lieutenant again and he'll chop you right off at the toes. You might be a good man, Chico, but against old Pappy Bressler you are way out of your class."

Chico looked sullen. "I still think it's wrong."

"It's the way the ball bounces." He slid in behind his desk, opened the bottom drawer, and pulled out a telephone directory. "Go on home. You've got a wife, don't you? Give her the pleasure of your company—or do you get testy with her too?"

"I'm not being testy," Chico growled. "I have a right to my opinion, don't I?"

"No. You gave up that right when you pinned on your badge. Being a cop is like being a dogface. Somebody tells you to take that hill and you go up. there and take it."

Chico's smile was bitter. "Ours not to reason why . . ."

"Now you've got it, Chico. There's hope for you yet."

Chico sat down in a chair facing the desk. He felt hollow inside, drained. He watched Harry flip through the pages of the telephone book.

"What are you doing?"

Harry glanced briefly at him. "Go home. You're off duty."

"You're up to something."

"You are so right. I am up to something. They may call me *Dirty* Harry, but no one has ever called me *Stupid* Harry." He closed the phone book with a snap, reached for the phone, and began to dial a number with swift strokes.

Chico chewed the bottom of his lip. "You need a backup man?"

Harry nodded curtly. "Frank Di Georgio is always available."

"I'm your partner."

"You're off duty—and you're tired."

"I can go a week without sleep."

"You're a big boy. I won't tell you what to do. If you want to stick around, that's your business."

"I want to stick around."

"OK, you're hired." The receiver was picked up on the other end of the line. Harry cupped a hand over the mouthpiece and spoke quietly. "Sid? Harry Callahan . . . yeah . . . sure . . . right as rain. How's by you? Good . . . need a little favor, Sid. OK? Fine . . .

73

be right down." He hung up. "It pays to have friends." He stood up and moved around the desk.

"Where are we going?"

Harry clucked his tongue in admonishment. "No questions, Chico. Just tag along, do as you're told, and keep your mouth shut."

He strode briskly across the room toward the hallway and Chico trailed after him. It felt good to Chico to be moving . . . to be doing something. He grinned at Bressler as he passed his office. The lieutenant did not grin back.

Sid Kleinman's electronics store was a cubbyhole on Grove Street near Alamo Square. He did not deal in street trade. It was not the kind of place one went to if the TV set needed a new tube or the radio was on the blink. But if you wanted to know who a certain senator talked to over his private phone, Sid Kleinman was the man you called for. There was a rumor that he had a bug on the hot line, but that was silly—or was it?

Harry and Chico were squeezed into a room that was wall-to-wall electronic gear. Kleinman, a gnomelike man in baggy gray pants and dirty carpet slippers, fussed away at a workbench that took up the better part of one wall. He swiveled around on a stool, plucked a jeweler's loupe from his right eye, and held up a tiny black box.

"Guaranteed . . . 100 percent."

Harry dropped the butt of a cigar on the floor and ground it to dust with his heel. "I'm not buying the damn thing."

Kleinman looked shocked. "Harry. Would I ask you for money? Would Sid Kleinman do such a thing to an old friend? No! It's yours for the asking. I only want you should know that you're getting the best . . . the *best!* Just bring it back in one piece and Sid Kleinman is the happiest man in the world."

"How does it work?"

"Believe me, a child would have no trouble. I pin the box inside your coat. The plug goes in your friend's ear. No wires . . . no little antenna . . . nothing. A plastic plug . . . like a hearing aid. You talk and he hears you. Up to three blocks. Don't shout or you'll deafen the man."

"How about tunnels?" Harry asked.

Sid Kleinman raised one shoulder and let it drop. "There is a limit to electronic miracles in so small a package. Keep in the open and everything will be hunky-dory."

"Hunky-dory," Harry repeated sourly.

"A Sid Kleinman guarantee!"

They tested the gadget on the street. It worked well up to four blocks if there were no big buildings in the way.

"That'll do it till six o'clock." Harry opened the glove compartment and placed the miniature sending set inside. "Go home and grab some sleep. Just be at the marina by nine o'clock. Use your own car. Wear jeans and a sweat shirt . . . tennis shoes. Be unobtrusive. This guy has a nose for cops so be nice and casual. OK?"

Chico nodded thoughtfully. "Should I carry a gun?"

Harry lit a cigar and blew the smoke toward the sky. "The department frowns on off-duty men packing firearms. No . . . don't carry a gun . . . leave it under the seat."

Two hundred thousand dollars in tens and twenties looks like a lot of money. It looks like two hundred thousand dollars' worth of slim, green bricks and it was a hell of a job fitting them into the suitcase that lay open on the chief of police's desk. A bespectacled young man from the mayor's office did the packing, fussing and fuming over it like a housewife trying to pack her husband's suitcase without wrinkling his shirts.

"There!" the man said triumphantly as he squeezed in the last bundle of twenties.

The chief glanced at Harry. "That's a lot of money. Don't let anybody take it away from you."

"I'll work on it," Harry replied dryly.

"You're all on your own. This man will contact you. He'll probably run you all over town to make sure you *are* alone. Go where he tells you to go. Do what he asks you to do. Play it by his rules. Nothing funny. You can defend yourself, but no overt aggressiveness. Is that understood?"

"It is."

"Deliver the ransom and report in. Period. If you have any questions, now's the time to ask them."

"Just one."

"What's that?"

"Where's your Scotch tape?"

The chief looked blank. "Top drawer . . . I suppose."

Harry walked around the desk, opened a drawer, and removed a roll of tape. He rolled up his right pant leg, took a six-inch black switchblade knife from the pocket of his jacket, and taped it firmly to the back of his calf. The chief grimaced.

"It's disgusting that a police officer of this city should know how to use a weapon like that."

Harry grinned wickedly. "I grew up on a tough block." He rolled down his pant leg, stamped his foot to make sure the knife was secure, picked up the suitcase, and walked out of the office. He looked like a brush salesman lugging his samples door to door.

The man from the mayor's office clucked his tongue. "He's certainly blasé about two hundred thousand dollars."

"Maybe," the chief agreed, "but I wouldn't want to be the man who made a grab for that case."

He was all alone. A hard, cold wind came off the bay and set the slim white boats in the marina to dancing. They bobbed around at their moorings like rubber ducks in a bathtub. Harry pulled up his coat collar and sat down on a bench facing the yacht basin. He placed the suitcase on the ground between his feet and looked casually about him. An elderly man and a small boy strolled by, the man holding the child's hand. The boy looked sullen and hostile.

"That there is a ketch, Albert . . . see . . . that white one over there."

"They're all white," the boy said. "All the boats are white."

"That's right, Albert—only this one has a blue deckhouse. See the one I mean? I'm pointing right at it."

"I wanna go home," the boy whined, "an' I want something to eat."

They wandered on, the old man taking his own sweet time, the boy dragging his feet beside him. When they were gone, the promenade stretched long and empty under the lights. Harry glanced at his watch. It was ten minutes before nine. He lit a cigar, picked up the suitcase, and wandered down to the end of the marina. There was a telephone booth there, a big bubble of plastic attached to a steel pole. Harry sat down on a bench within jumping distance of the phone. Reaching inside his jacket, he pressed the side of the little box that was pinned there.

"I'm waiting," he said. "I hope to hell you can hear me, Chico. I hope to hell you're *there*. You wouldn't oversleep, would you, Chico?"

Three blocks away Chico Gonsales smiled as the voice of Harry Callahan tinkled faintly in his ear. He sat in his car, which was parked in front of a chicken takeout stand.

"I won't talk anymore, Chico. There's a fisherman coming. At least, he looks like a fisherman. He's got a fishing rod . . . but what the hell does that prove?"

"That's right, Harry," Chico said to himself, "don't trust anybody."

77

The man was a fisherman. He ignored Harry as he went through an elaborate ritual of tying on hooks, putting on bait, attaching lead weights and a bobble float before casting out into the dark water.

It was nine o'clock.

VI

RRRRIIIINNNNNGGGGG . . .
RRRRIIIINNNNNGGGGG . . .
Harry grabbed the phone before it rang again.
"Hello?"
There was silence on the other end but he could hear
heavy breathing. Finally, a voice, a quiet, friendly
sounding voice. "Do you have a suitcase?"
"Right beside me."
"What's your name, mister?"
"Callahan."
"Just Callahan?"
"Harry Francis."
"Do you like that name, Harry Francis Callahan?"
"I'm stuck with it."
There was a moment's pause. Then: "I don't have a
name. Don't you think that's better? Wouldn't you real-
ly prefer not to have a name?"
Harry was starting to sweat. Jesus, he thought, get
the hell on with it.
"I don't know," he said tautly. "I've never thought
about it."
"What are you? I mean, what do you do?"
"I'm a police officer."
The silence became leaden. When the man spoke

again, his voice was harsher. There was an edge to it and Harry could sense the hate. It came through the wires with palpable force.

"All right, *cop*. Pay attention. I say nothing twice. Here's the way we go about it. I bounce you around a bit to make sure you're alone. I put a time limit from phone booth to phone booth. I ring four times. You don't answer—I hang up and that's the end of the game. That's all she wrote, *cop*. The girl dies."

"Is the girl all right?"

"You're dumb. You know that, *cop?* You're a dumb pig bastard. *Is the girl all right?* What kind of dumb question is that?"

Harry struggled to keep his voice steady. "We're not paying a nickel for a corpse."

"Shut up! Just shut up and listen. The girl's breathing. She keeps on breathing till three in the morning. Just remember that, *cop*. Just keep that in your pig mind. You do what I tell you. If I even *think* you're being followed by any of your pig friends, the girl dies. You talk to anyone, the girl dies. You so much as bend down to pat a goddamn dog, the girl dies. You got that?"

"I've got it."

"That's good. That's very good. Now, you listen to me. I'll be watching you. Not all the time, but you'll never know when or where. No car. You walk . . . run . . . crawl . . . but you be at Scott and Bay in ten minutes . . . the gas station . . . four rings or forget it. Understand?"

"Yes."

"Cop . . . I hope you're not dumb."

There was a soft click and then the dial tone. Harry slammed down the receiver, picked up the suitcase, and started to run.

"Scott and Bay, Chico!"

He could only pray Chico was hearing him. He ran hard, startling the strollers on the boulevard as he raced out of the marina and headed toward Scott Street.

He jostled a man as he crossed Jefferson and the man swung angrily about, shouting at him to watch where he was going.

It took exactly ten minutes to reach the corner of Bay and Scott and Harry's breath was coming in gasps as he came into the bright circles of light flooding the service station. The telephone booth was at the far edge of the asphalt parkway and it started to ring just as Harry reached it.

"Callahan!" he croaked.

"Funston playground . . . corner of Laguna . . . fifteen minutes."

CLICK

Harry was off and running.

"Hey! What's the hurry, fella?" one of the attendants called after him.

Harry did not hear him. All that he could hear was the blood beating in his brain. The suitcase tugged at his arm like a ton of paving stones. Two hundred thousand dollars. He would gladly have tossed it away for ten cents. Every muscle and nerve in his right arm shrieked for relief. But there was to be no relief. Sweat ran in scalding streams down his forehead and burned his eyes by the time he reached the battered, graffiti-etched phone booth at Funston playground. The phone rang three times before he reached it, but he snatched the receiver before the fourth ring.

"Callahan!" The word came out like a gasp of pain.

"How do you feel, *cop?*"

"Fine."

"You feel like death, you fat pig. Now keep running . . . Aquatic Park . . . east end Fort Mason tunnel . . . twenty minutes."

CLICK

Harry transferred the case to his left hand and ran down Laguna toward the gloom of Fort Mason.

"Chico," he blurted as he ran, "you won't be . . . able to . . . pick me up . . . in tunnel . . . cruise Beach . . . Larkin . . ."

81

He cursed Sid Kleinman for not having given him a two-way communications system. He was running in the dark, talking to the wind. A woman walking down Laguna, hurrying past the dark shadows of the playground, backed off in terror as Harry raced toward her, his face contorted in pain, his lips moving, talking to himself. He swung the case back to his right hand. The muscles protested and he nearly dropped it. He gritted his teeth and held on, kept running, his left leg starting to protest now, the barely healed shotgun wound beginning to open. He tried to favor the leg. He was running like a cripple. His lungs were brass. The killer had been right—he felt like death.

The Fort Mason tunnel yawned ahead of him, long, dark, and deserted. He looked quickly at his watch as he ran beneath a light pole. He had ten minutes.

"Oh, Jesus."

It was too much for his body to bear. He slowed to a walk as he entered the tunnel, relishing the cool wind that blew through it from Aquatic Park at the far end. The wind dried the sweat on his face, but it made his damp shirt feel like a coating of ice against his chest. A chill swept over him and he shuddered.

"Run," he said, "run, you bastard—run." He shifted his grip on the leather handle and started to trot, the suitcase banging against his leg with every step. He was no longer carrying it, he was lugging it along like a ball and chain.

There were recessed lights in the tunnel walls and they cast dim squares of yellow on the concrete floor. Between the yellow squares there was nothing but deep shadow. The tunnel curved, and as Harry rounded it, he saw movement in the shadows. Shapes were stirring at the fringe of light, fanning out, blocking the way. He slowed to a walk as the shadows assumed shapes—four big, hulking youths . . . poised . . . waiting.

"What's in the bag, dad?" One of them stepped away from the group. He was wearing skintight jeans, a dirty

T-shirt, and jackboots. A beard struggled to grow on his young, tough face. "I said what's in the bag?"

"Screw the bag," another one said, shifting slowly toward Harry's right. "Screw the fuckin' bag. Let's have your wallet, daddy."

Harry let the suitcase fall at his feet. "Don't hurt me," he whined, unbuttoning his jacket, slipping his right hand inside.

The boys laughed, their laughter low, lacking mirth, a deep rumbling sound echoing through the tunnel.

"The wallet, pops . . . let's have the wallet."

"Anything you say, *sonny!*" The big magnum was out of its holster and in his hand quicker than the eye could follow. He pressed the muzzle flush into the young hood's face.

"Blow," he said.

The boys backed off, but the gun in Harry's hand never wavered.

"Screw it," one of them muttered and began to run. The others followed, down the tunnel toward Fort Mason, their boots ringing on the concrete.

Harry swore under his breath as he slipped the gun back in the holster. He had lost precious minutes. Time was running out on him. He grabbed up the suitcase and ran like a maniac toward the distant patch of light that marked the Aquatic Park exit.

RRRRIIIINNNNGGGG . . .

RRRRIIIINNNNGGGG . . .

RRRRIIIINNNNGGGG . . .

He could hear the telephone as he burst out of the tunnel. The phone was attached to the side of a hamburger stand on the breakwater. An old man was standing near it, lowering the iron shutters over the front of the counter. He moved to the phone, reaching for it on the fourth ring.

"No!" Harry shouted. "Don't answer that!"

The man ignored the shouts. "Hello. What do you want?"

Harry snatched the instrument out of the man's hand.

"Callahan!"

There was only silence—except for the spluttering outrage of the old man.

"I said, *Callahan!*"

"I heard you," the voice replied with quiet menace. "Who picked it up?"

"An old man. I never saw him before."

"You're a liar."

CLICK

Harry slumped against the side of the stand. "Christ, Chico . . . he hung up on me." He replaced the receiver and leaned back against the wall, sucking wind.

The old man was still spluttering, his words slurred by his lack of teeth. He was mad as a wet owl.

"Take it easy," Harry breathed, "you'll live longer."

RRRRIIIINNNNGGGG . . .

Harry whirled to the phone. "CALLAHAN!"

"Don't shout," the voice said. "Don't you ever raise your voice to me again."

"I'm sorry." He meant it. He was begging and it was obvious.

"All right, I believe you. The stand's closing, isn't it? The old man's shuttering up the place. Don't bother to look around. I'm not watching you now. The old man has his habits. It's my hobby to study habits. You're a cop. You get around. You've seen that hamburger stand before. You lied about the old man. You must have seen him a hundred times. You just never bothered to notice him."

"You're right. I have seen him."

"That's better. We have to be honest. I'm a Scorpio, you know. I trust people and I expect people to be honest with me."

"I'm being honest . . . believe me."

"I believe you. Do you know Mount Davidson Park?"

"Of course . . . sure."

"Go there. Go to the cross."

"That's a hell of a walk."

"Take a streetcar. Get off at Forest Hills station. You

84

can walk from there. It won't kill you." He hung up quietly.

So we're coming to the end of the trail, Harry thought. Mount Davidson Park. He didn't know what he would find under the giant cross on the hill but the gun under his arm was a distinct comfort.

It was a long ride, but he was grateful to be sitting down. He stared out the window as the streetcar racketed across town, into the subway, under the bowels of Twin Peaks. His face stared back at him from the dusty window, hard under the lights, a bleak face, worn and haggard.

And he thought:

God, who is this guy? What the hell am I up against? That soft, prissy little voice . . . then all that steel . . . that cold hate. What the hell kind of guy is he? No name. Scorpio. Jesus.

And he worried:

What if Chico isn't around? What if the whole thing goes sour? This guy is a gunman. He could snipe me as I came up the hill. He's got a silencer on that rifle. Chico could be twenty yards away and he wouldn't hear a thing . . . not a motherin' thing.

A drunk sailor slouched into the seat beside him. His eyes were glassy.

"I gotta be at Hunter's Point in half an hour. OK, buddy? Jus' do me a little ol' favor. Press the button."

"You're on the wrong car," Harry said.

"That a fact?" The sailor closed his eyes. His head rolled to one side and he was asleep, his legs turning to straw. He looked like a stuffed sailor doll tossed in a corner.

"Forest Hills Station!" the conductor shouted. "Forest Hills!"

It was five minutes after eleven when Harry reached the edge of the park. He looked up at the black hill, the mountain of Davidson, with the floodlit cross soaring a hundred feet or more into the night sky.

"Chico. I'm on Juanita between Rex and Del Sur now. I'm going into the park . . . up to the cross by the quickest route. I won't contact you again unless I see something. Don't follow too close. Move up the opposite way . . . Molimo Drive or Coventry Lane. Stay alert, you siesta-loving bastard."

And then he was across the road and into the trees—heading for the high ground—a suitcase-toting dogface cop.

The paths were spider trails gray with starlight. Every clump of brush was a killer, every tree limb a rifle barrel. There were footsteps on the path behind him, moving quickly, gaining on him. Harry looked back to see the tall figure of a man silhouetted against the lights of the city. The man hesitated a second and then came slowly, hesitantly, up the path toward him.

Harry held the suitcase in his left hand, his right tensed, ready to dive for the magnum. "I'm Callahan," he said clearly.

The man paused and began to giggle. "My friends call me Alice. And I *will* take a dare."

Harry grinned and relaxed. "When did you get busted last, *Alice?*"

The man quivered and waved thin, pale hands. "Oh, shit. If you're Vice I'll kill myself."

"You do that."

The man melted back into the darkness and Harry waited until he heard the sound of his footsteps fade in the distance. He continued on, up the steep path, half running now, hurrying upward toward the cross—hurrying toward God knew what.

It was a spot for lovers, up there on the top of the city, the top of the world. A secluded place, sanctified somehow by the cross. Not a favorite place for the casual necker. Like doing it in the back row of a church. On soft summer nights it was a place for whispered vows and the giving of rings. No one was up there now but a breathless Harry Callahan leaning against the concrete base of the cross. Only Harry Callahan on top of the world—with one other man.

"Freeze."

The voice came out of the blackness and the wispy tendrils of mist. It came like a cold wind.

"Freeze, you son of a bitch. Hold it like a fuckin' statue. You move an eyebrow and I'll chop you in half."

The man with no name moved out of the bushes like a cat stalking a bird. He wore tan chino pants and a brown windbreaker, white cotton gloves on his hands. A nylon stocking was pulled over his head, the mesh squashing his features, turning them into an obscene blur. He held a rifle-butted Schmeisser machine pistol, nine-millimeter *Schutzstaffel* issue, in his hands, the slim barrel pointing directly at Harry's groin.

"Harry Francis Callahan?"

Harry said nothing. The machine pistol moved in a nasty arc.

"Answer me, pig!"

"Harry Francis Callahan." His voice sounded alien.

"That's more like it. What I ask you to do, you *do*. Is that understood?"

"Yes."

"Put the bag down . . . slowly."

Harry put the bag down, slowly.

"Left hand, nice and easy. Let's see your gun—and don't tell me you haven't got one."

Harry opened his jacket with his left hand and pulled it back to reveal the shoulder holster and the big black butt of the Smith and Wesson.

"My, my, that's a big one. Pull it out with your pinky and toss it away."

Harry drew out the gun with his little finger and made a clumsy toss. The gun hit the grass six feet away and Harry marked the spot in his mind.

"Now up with the hands . . . high, very, very high."

He raised his hands high. He was playing it straight down the line.

"Turn around, face the cement, hands out and spread 'em. You know the drill."

Harry did as he was told. He faced the concrete and rested his forehead against it. His hands were pushing the smoothly troweled surface and his feet were spread apart in the neatly clipped grass. He was a model of cooperation—no trouble to the man at all. There was no reason for the man to come up behind him, raise the barrel of the Schmeisser, and hammer it down on the back of Harry's neck. No reason at all—but he did it anyway. Harry hit the grass like a barrel of sand, rolled onto his back, and lay with his face to the sky, to the stars that he could not see.

Chico had cursed the plastic receiver from the moment he had first placed it in his ear. It hummed and buzzed like an agitated bee. It was annoying as hell, but he didn't dare take it out for even a second. It picked up sound all right, but faintly and garbled. "Scott and Bay, Chico," had come out as "Dotan Day, Bico."

But he had figured it out. He had kept within four blocks of Harry's circuitous route all the way to Mount Davidson park. He had been on Portola Drive when Harry had informed him he was going up to the cross. He had scorched a little rubber off the rear tires as he careened off the broad avenue and raced down Marne onto Dalewood Way. He took an unpaved caretaker's road deep into the park, drew up under some eucalyptus trees, took his revolver out of the glove compartment, and continued up the narrowing road on foot.

Now he worked his way up the back of a steep hill, avoiding the footpaths. Brush tore at him and thick groves of low trees swallowed him in inky, insect-humming darkness. The illuminated cross guided him, but it never seemed to get any closer.

A sudden jumble of words, terribly faint, hummed in his ear. He couldn't make out anything clearly but the sound gave him a boost. Harry was close, not over five hundred yards up the mountain. An arroyo yawned at his feet. Five hundred yards! Five hundred *miles* through the bush.

He squatted on his heels, the machine pistol resting across his knees, staring into the face of Harry Francis Callahan.

"Wake up, you son of a bitch." His voice was soft, strangely gentle. He raised his right arm lazily and back-handed Harry across the mouth. Harry's head snapped to one side and he opened his eyes, groaning with pain.

The man rose slowly to his feet, eyed Harry critically for a few seconds, then cocked a foot and punted him squarely in the groin. Harry jackknifed with pain; a scream ripping his throat. The lower part of his body felt like broken glass. He clutched himself between the legs and the man kicked him in the hands.

"You scream again and I'll blow your face off! You just keep that pig mouth shut and you listen to me. I've got things to tell you, cop, and you're not paying any attention. Are you? Goddamn it, answer me!"

Harry stared at him, his eyes like marble balls. The man leaned over and brought the butt of the gun down hard on Harry's throat, just below the Adam's apple. Harry vomited and turned his head to one side to keep from drowning in his own wastes.

The man grimaced with disgust, gripped Harry by the hair and shook his head the way a dog shakes a rat.

"Pig! Dirty, filthy bastard! You listen to me, crud mouth, because I'm not finished with you yet. I've got something to tell you. Can you hear me?"

Harry only gurgled. The man released the grip on his hair and slugged him on the temple with his fist.

"I said . . . *can you hear me?*"

"Yes." The word bubbled out of yellow froth, barely audible.

"That's better, because I want you to know something before I kick your kidneys to pulp. There's been a little change in plans. *The girl dies.*"

There is a deep, raw nerve in every man that is better

89

left untouched, for to do so is to unleash a primeval and terrible savagery. An inarticulate sound came from Harry Callahan: the howl of a maddened beast, cornered and ready to die—for a price. Harry reached up with his hand and clawed at the killer's throat, ripping at it with his nails, seeking the blood beneath the skin. Something red and ugly was exploding in his brain, stripping every vestige of civilization away from him. He wanted to dig his fingers into the jugular and rip it from the man's throat. He wanted to claw flesh. He wanted to drink blood. He wanted to do a lot of things, but his strength had ebbed. His taut fingers were little more than a caress.

"You're pathetic," the man said. He slapped Harry's hand away with the barrel of the gun and stood up, working the bolt mechanism, cranking a shell into the chamber. He backed slowly away, bringing the butt of the Schmeisser up to his shoulder. He took careful aim at Harry's chest.

"You're going to bleed, cop. You're going to bleed like a fuckin' pig."

BLAM ... BLAM ...

The shots came one after the other, as quickly as a finger could press twice on a trigger. The slugs howled skyward, not meant for anyone, but they sent the killer spinning to one side, hurling his body into the tall, wet ferns that bordered the base of the cross. He hit the ground with the gun poised and ready, the lever flicked to semiautomatic fire. He lay prone in the greenery, cursing the floodlights that bathed his position like a star shell, and slowly traversed the shadow line of brush at the edge of the grass from where he knew the shots had come. He had lost all interest in the sprawled figure of Harry Francis Callahan. He aimed low at the brush line and slowly, carefully, squeezed off four shots. The slim gun jumped in his hands and the bullets clipped the scrub and whined across the arroyo. The shots flushed Chico out of the bushes. He broke cover and ran along the edge of the grass toward a stone drinking fountain, firing from the hip as he ran, his bullets slapping into the concrete base of the cross and howling off in ricochet.

The killer flipped the firing lever to fully automatic and sent the nine shots left in the clip rattling at the fleeing figure. The stream of bullets cut divots out of the turf and tore chunks of concrete and stone out of the drinking fountain but they failed to hit Chico Gonsales.

"Bastard!" the killer screamed. He had one more clip fastened to the inside of his windbreaker, but it was too awkward to get at while lying prone in the ferns. He backed off like a crab and worked his way toward the far side of the towering concrete base. A slug from Chico's gun followed him, whining a few inches above his head.

"Chico! No! Don't kill him!" It took every scrap of energy Harry could muster to shout so loudly. He nearly choked with the strain and deep, lung-shaking coughs tore at him.

"OK, *compadre!*" Chico shouted back. He lay flat behind the comforting shield of the drinking fountain. He could see the killer working his way toward the edge of the base. In another few seconds he would be around it and out of sight. He had time for one more shot, but the distance was great. He couldn't guarantee a wound. He lowered his gun, swearing softly to himself. He would have to work his way around to the mall at the north side of the cross and then try and rush the guy. It was a hell of a risk but he knew it was the only way.

Harry crawled painfully across the grass, hands outstretched, groping like a blind man. He felt wet grass, fern, twigs, small stones, but not the solid heft of the Smith and Wesson. It was lying somewhere, but *where?* He felt totally disoriented. He shook his head numbly, rested, took several deep drafts of cold, misty air, and felt better.

"To hell with it," he breathed harshly. Reaching down to his leg he plucked the switchblade away from his calf, pressed the button, and murmured his satisfaction as the six-inch blade flashed wickedly into sight.

The killer tossed the spent clip into the ferns and clicked the full one into place. He cocked the gun, placed it in the crook of his arms, and started to crawl rapidly along the base of the cross toward Callahan and the suitcase. The money was uppermost in his mind. Callahan he would kill with one quick shot in the brain. He would grab the suitcase and get into the tall brush. If the other cop was stupid enough to follow him—well, that was his tough luck.

BLAM   BLAM   BLAM

Chico broke from the mall firing as he came, shooting well above the killer's head. He stopped halfway across the sweep of lawn, held his revolver with both hands, and leveled it straight and true.

"Toss the gun out! Quick! You're covered, so don't try anything!"

The killer rolled to one side, swinging the machine pistol outward, snapping off one shot. The bullet caught Chico high up on the right shoulder, splintering his clavicle like a dry twig. The force of the impact slammed him to the ground, his revolver going off as he fell, the bullet searing a long groove across the grass.

"So long, *cop!*" the killer called out exultantly. Rising quickly, he wedged the butt of the gun into his shoulder and brought it to bear on Chico who was trying to crawl toward the cover of some brush. He had a good twenty yards to go and the killer was taking his time, aiming at a point just ahead of Chico's head, enjoying himself as he waited for Chico to crawl into the line of sight.

He waited a second too long.

Harry Callahan, crawling painfully across the grass, lunged upward with the knife and buried it to the hilt in the man's left leg five inches below the hipbone.

92

"Mother of Christ!"

Harry held onto the handle and tried to draw the knife out for another stab, but his hand slipped and he only succeeded in twisting the blade in the wound.

"Help me!"

Nothing existed but the pain. The man clawed at the knife, letting the gun fall at his feet. He ran toward the gloom of the trees, dragging the wounded leg behind him. He passed the suitcase without looking at it and did not stop running until he was deep in the shrubs at the bottom of the arroyo. He leaned back against an outcropping of rock and tugged at the knife with trembling hands. It slid out easily and he could feel a rush of hot, sticky blood pour over his fingers.

"You bastard," he said thickly. "You dirty rotten bastard."

He glanced up at the crest of the hill. He could see the top section of the cross, glaring white under spotlights. He cursed that too, then wound his way downward through the thick brush toward the city far below.

VII

It was one fifteen in the morning.

Harry lay on the battered leather couch in Lieutenant Bressler's office staring at the wall clock through the glass partition.

One sixteen.

The lieutenant was on the telephone, cupping the mouthpiece with his hand, his voice low and solemn.

"It could have been a hell of a lot worse, chief . . . sure . . . sure I can understand how the mayor feels about it . . . sure . . . sure, first thing in the morning." He hung up and swung slowly back and forth in his chair.

One seventeen.

"It all hit the fan down at City Hall."

"Yeah?" Harry tore his eyes away from the clock.

"You know how it is . . . the mayor leans on the chief and the chief leans on me."

"Don't lean on *me*, Al. I'm not in the mood." His voice was a whisper of menace.

Bressler shifted uncomfortably in his seat. "You oughta be in a hospital. Christ, you look like you were run over by a truck."

"You're changing the subject, Al. Who are you phoning first thing in the morning—his honor?"

"Yes. He wants to know if the department didn't understand his orders. Meaning, are we just plain stupid or did we deliberately disobey him? He wants to know why Gonsales was up there—something I'm curious about myself, by the way. To be brief, he wants to know why we screwed it up, Harry."

"We didn't. Scorpio screwed it. The whole thing was a con."

"We only have your word."

"Do you doubt it?"

"No. You know me better than that. Hell, I know *you*. But it looks bad from the mayor's angle. It looks like a botched job. It looks like Gonsales's being around screwed up the works."

"If Chico hadn't been around, you'd be talking to a goddamn *wall* right now."

It was hopeless. He looked at the clock.

One nineteen.

"You're not on the wagon, are you, Al?"

Bressler sighed deeply and got reluctantly to his feet. There was a portable refrigerator in one corner of the room—a Christmas gift from the department two years before. Bressler opened it and took out a cold bottle of vodka.

"You want some vermouth in it?"

"I just want a drink, not a party."

Bressler poured three fingers into a water glass and handed it to him.

Harry sat up and sipped the vodka, letting it trickle soothingly down his bruised throat.

"You just tell the mayor it was my idea. I gave Gonsales orders as a superior. You didn't know a damn thing about it. Tell him he can have my badge."

"Now, Harry—"

"I mean it, Al. He can have it with a red rose on it. I'll deliver it in person. I'd appreciate the opportunity of telling him a few things. The whole operation was a barrel of crud right from the start. The mayor panicked and he passed that panic right down the line. Kidnapping's a *federal* crime, Al. Or didn't his honor know that? There should have been feds all over that park, like squirrels."

"Well . . ."

"Don't make excuses. You're too good a cop for that."

One twenty-three.

The phone rang, sharply persistent in the quiet room. Bressler picked it up. "Yeah, speaking. Who? OK . . . put him on." He looked over at Harry with grim expectancy. "A doctor at Golden Gate Emergency . . . sounds like a payoff."

Within minutes after Harry and Chico had been picked up by the Mount Davidson Park patrol, Harry had been on the radio with a description of the killer and his condition. A knife thrust in the leg is no small matter and Bressler reasoned that the man might seek help. All hospitals were alerted, as well as all night drug stores and half a dozen doctors known by the police to have underworld connections. Now, at one twenty-five, the groundwork was bearing fruit. A doctor at the twenty-four-hour emergency hospital on the fringe of Haight-Ashbury was calling in about a patient . . . about thirty years old . . . medium build . . . sallow complexion . . . tan chino pants and brown windbreaker . . . a deep puncture wound in the upper left thigh.

Harry and Frank Di Georgio were down there in ten minutes.

The doctor was no longer young. He had the look of a man who had spent half his lifetime gazing on the misery of others. A good deal of that misery was reflected in his eyes as he looked at Harry and Di Georgio.

"We get lots of stabbings here," he said. His voice was tired and heavily European. "Junkies . . . speed freaks . . . they stab one another . . . they don't know what they're doing. This man was not a junkie. I could tell by his eyes. He came in alone. He said he had had an accident. I looked at the wound and I knew it was not so. One does not make such a wound in an accidental manner. It was clear to the femur. I knew he was lying to me, so I asked him to wait for a minute and

96

came in here to call the police. When I came out, the man was gone."

"Did he give you his name?" Harry asked.

The doctor smiled thinly. "No—but that did not matter. If they give you a name, it is never *their* name. But . . . there was something about the man . . ."

"Anything you can think of, doctor. It's very important that we find him before 3 A.M."

"Yes. Well . . . I have seen him before. I am sure of that. But where?" He stared thoughtfully at the ceiling, his fingers tapping the scarred wood of his desk. There was a big clock on the wall behind him, the red sweep second hand moving relentlessly on.

It lacked fifteen seconds before 2 A.M.

"Doctor. For Christ's sake, try to remember!"

"I'm trying . . . I seem to recall . . . yes. Yes!" He stood up, pointing toward the window. "Football. When they had the football. He used to sell programs at the stadium. The groundskeeper let him live there. Perhaps he still does."

"Let him live where?" Di Georgio asked.

"There!" the doctor cried, still pointing toward the window. "At Kezar Stadium."

Di Georgio floored the gas pedal and the police car rocketed across the vast, empty parking lot. He hit the brakes hard as the towering iron mesh fence loomed up in the headlights, and the car skidded to a halt in front of the west gate. Beyond the gate the tiered concrete oval of the stadium receded in the darkness.

"There's a lock on the gate big as a barrel," Di Georgio said.

"To hell with the lock. We go up and over."

Di Georgio frowned. "We don't have a warrant, Harry."

"We don't have any time, either," Harry snapped. He got out of the car and looked up at the fence. "Think you can make it, Frank?"

Di Georgio tapped his paunch. "Not in a million

years. I'll drive around toward the east gate. I'll find a way in."

Harry started up the wire, wedging the toes of his shoes between the links. Every move of his legs sent a stab of pain through his groin. The fence seemed three miles high, but he made it over the top and down the other side, dropping the last few feet. He started off at a trot toward the long tunnel that sliced under the stadium and came out on the playing field. Doors led off from that tunnel into a labyrinth of corridors and rooms. One of the rooms would be the groundskeeper's. All he had to do was to find it.

He moved cautiously into the tunnel with his gun drawn. The tunnel was like an echo chamber and his footsteps rang hollowly in the terrible silence. He cursed the sound and continued on tiptoe. A few low-wattage bulbs set into the wall behind iron grids threw some light, just enough to read the markings on the doors:

DELIVERY ONLY
NO. 12 STORAGE ROOM—KEEP OUT
ACME CONCESSIONS, INC.

and, finally, near the end of the tunnel:

GROUNDSKEEPER—PRIVATE

Harry paused in front of it. A simple wooden door. A crack of light around it. It could have been open—it could have been locked; he did not try the handle. Lifting his right foot, he kicked the door open with a splintering crash and bulled his way into the room beyond.

It was empty and there was no place to hide. It was not so much a room as it was a cell; a cold, featureless place where a man did nothing but sleep and eat. There was a canvas cot along one wall, a small table, and one wooden chair against another. A hot plate stood on a shelf above the table, glowing cherry red, a battered

aluminum coffee pot standing on it, pouring steam.
Harry flipped the plug out of the wall and looked
around. If the killer had any clothes, they were on his
back. There was no closet, no chest of drawers. The
only object that linked him to the room lay on the floor
under the cot—a cheap brown suitcase.

Harry picked it up and placed it on the table. He
flicked up the catches with one hand and opened the
lid. The pieces of a thirty-thirty rifle lay inside, each
section resting snugly in cut-out styrofoam.

"The clever son of a bitch," Harry murmured.

He had come back like a wounded dog to its kennel.
He had put on the coffee but before he could drink any
he must have heard the ring of Harry's footsteps coming
down the tunnel. Harry stiffened, straining his ears in
the tomblike silence, listening for the slightest reverber-
ation. It came suddenly, almost directly above him, the
unmistakable sound of footsteps moving rapidly over
concrete.

Harry darted from the room and ran on down the
tunnel. A flight of concrete steps rose in shadowed tiers
toward the upper level. Harry took them two at a time,
ignoring the jolts of pain that shot through his pelvis as
he ran. He reached the first level with its line of shuttered concession booths along the inner wall facing rows
of box seats that sloped down toward the black oval of
the playing field. The stadium was awesome in its empti-
ness. It could seat fifty-nine thousand people. Somewhere among all those seats cowered one slender man.

Harry walked on, keeping close to the shuttered
booths. The magnum was getting heavy in his hand and
he brought it up across his chest, bracing it with his left
palm. Something stirred among the seats and a white
shape rose into the wind, wings beating as it struggled
for height.

Harry cursed the seagull, silently and vehemently. He
leaned back against a shutter, his heart pounding. The
killer had left a thirty-thirty custom-made rifle in his
room. He had left a Nazi machine pistol in Mount

Davidson Park. What else did he have in his arsenal?
Hand grenades?

He scanned the endless rows of seats, the dark middle
ground. The bastard was someplace—but where? He
ducked down one of the rows and knelt on the cold
concrete beside the low wood partition of a section of
boxes.

"You're covered! Hold it right there!" His voice
bounced around in the shell of the stadium and seemed
to come from all directions at the same time. There was
a flurry of movement far down toward the fifty-yard
line. A man was running down the aisle toward the
field, running badly, sloppily, his left leg trailing gro-
tesquely. Harry fired, shooting deliberately high, the
bullet screaming into the gloom. It did not slow up the
runner. Harry took after him, running along the top of
the benches, leaping the aisles. He slammed full tilt into
a row of seats but kept on running, oblivious to the
sharp pain in his hip. The killer had clambered over the
low fence that separated the seats from the field. He was
on the oval cinder track, his body a vague white shape
in the inky expanse of turf.

Inspector Di Georgio found an opening in the fence
low enough and wide enough for him to get through. He
sprinted heavily toward the stadium, broke a window,
and clambered into the maintenance section. He floun-
dered through the catacombs under the stadium, heard
the sound of a shot reverberate through the corridors of
concrete and began to run around like a rat caught in
a maze. The passageway he was in ended at a small
green door marked:

MASTER ELECTRICAL CONTROLS
ALL UNAUTHORIZED PERSONNEL KEEP OUT

The door was padlocked. Di Georgio blew the lock to
pieces with two shots, bounded inside the dimly lit room,

and pulled the master switch. High above him great banks of floodlights snapped on.

The killer stopped on the center markings of the twenty-yard line as the playing field turned bright as day. He was frozen by the glare, paralyzed by the brilliance. Harry Callahan felt no such consternation. Vaulting the low fence, he walked slowly, calmly, across the wet grass, holding his gun with both hands. The killer waited for him. He carried no weapon other than his two clawed hands. He stood stiffly . . . waiting . . . a jungle animal backed into a corner. Twenty yards from him, Harry dropped to one knee and took careful, deliberate aim, then slapped a bullet into the man's leg two inches below the knife wound. The force of the forty-four slug kicked the leg out from under him and he fell heavily to the ground, twisting and flailing on the grass.

Harry walked over to him and stood looking down at the writhing, pain-racked figure. He felt nothing.

"Where is she?"

The killer looked up at him with haunted eyes. "Get me a doctor. Jesus . . . mother . . . get me a doctor."

"Where is she, punk?"

"I'm bleeding to death, you bastard."

"Where's the girl?"

"A doctor . . . please . . . get me a doctor."

"Where is she?"

The killer shifted his tortured gaze from Harry's cold, implacable face.

"I want a lawyer," he mumbled. "I got a right to a lawyer."

"I'm going to keep asking. I'm going to keep asking you where the girl is, and you know something, punk? You're going to tell me."

The killer screwed his lips and tried to spit up into Harry's face. It was a last, futile gesture of defiance. Harry stuck out his right foot and placed the heel of his shoe on the bleeding gunshot wound. He pressed down hard, grinding his heel into the wound the way a man might grind out a cigarette on the sidewalk. The killer screamed until there was not enough breath left in his body to work up another one. Then he sagged limply on the grass, staring at the dark sky, his face the color of wet chalk.

Harry raised his foot and placed his bloody heel over the knife wound. The killer whimpered, looking up at him in stark terror.

"Well?" Harry's voice was thin, like the edge of a razor. "You ready to talk now? Or do I do another dance on your leg?"

It was going to be a beautiful day, the type of day that would set the pulses of the chamber of commerce men racing and justify all their hyperbole about San Francisco weather. But none of the men on the promontory bothered to glance toward the eastern sky. They stood under portable lights watching a dozen firemen dig furiously into the soft soil at the tip of Fort Point.

"We've found it!" one of them shouted. He tossed his shovel to one side and reached down into the hole, hands brushing loose earth from the corner of a cardboard box. A hole was punched carefully through the cardboard and a flexible rubber hose attached to a bottle of oxygen was pushed into it.

"We'll have it up in two minutes!" came an excited shout.

Harry Callahan stood apart from the others, leaning against the fender of a squad car, chewing an unlit cigar. The portable lights cast crazy, elongated shadows and made the firemen seem like ghouls robbing a grave.

Well, he thought, that's what they're doing, isn't it?

The top of the large carton was revealed and sliced open with infinite care. A hard, white light was trained down as the top was lifted off. Inside, curled into the carton like a bloody embryo, was the body of a young, naked girl, the body of Mary Ann Deacon—a long time dead.

A grim-faced Lieutenant Bressler followed the blanket-shrouded body of the girl to the doors of the waiting ambulance. He watched as the young doctor from General Hospital placed the body carefully, almost reverently, on the bed and signaled the driver to take off. He stood bareheaded in the fresh dawn wind and watched the ambulance drive slowly up the narrow dirt road toward the Presidio, then he walked back to his car where Harry Callahan stood waiting.

"It was all a con," Harry said softly. "Wasn't it, Al?"

Bressler looked at Harry for a moment, then fished into his pocket, brought out a silver lighter, and lit Harry's cigar with it.

"The doc said she'd been dead for at least twenty hours. She may have been breathing when he stuck her in that soap carton, but not a hell of a lot longer. It's a rotten case, Harry."

"They all are," Harry said. He puffed on his cigar for a moment, then dropped it at his feet and ground it to dust. "Let's go back to the office, Al. Let's wrap this bastard up."

Harry worked all day on the arrest report, keeping himself going with black coffee, cigars, and peanut butter sandwiches. He snatched an hour's snooze on Bressler's couch and spent ten minutes talking to Chico in the hospital . . .

A snapped clavicle? A piece of cake. Came out the back? You've got a conversation piece, boy. Enjoy it! . . . but Chico had sounded depressed and not in the mood for jokes. The bullet that hit him had mushroomed after striking the clavicle and had cracked into the scapula about as neatly as a hammer hitting a dried gourd. He was crippled and in pain and not above saying so.

Well, just hang in there, kid.

Talking to Chico had not been the high point of Harry's day. He had always been bad news for partners . . . Fanduchi dead . . . Sam out of it with a hole in his lung . . . that kid Joey whatever-his-name-was who had lasted one day. Bad news. He tried to get his mind off Chico and went back to work. By three in the afternoon the report of the arrest and capture of Scorpio, a John Doe, by Inspector Harry Francis Callahan, Homicide Division, San Francisco Police Department, was typed, signed, and on its way to the office of William T. Rothko, district attorney.

The persistent ringing of the telephone woke Harry at nine o'clock the following morning. Bressler had given him the day off and his first inclination was just to let the damn thing ring until whoever was on the other end grew tired of hanging on, but after the tenth ring Harry reached out of bed and picked up the phone.

"Inspector Callahan?" A woman's voice, crisp but pleasant.

"Speaking."

"This is Miss Willis in the district attorney's office. Mr. Rothko would like to see you as soon as possible. He said it was quite urgent. What time shall I tell him you'll be in, inspector?"

Harry groaned inwardly. "After I shave. Make it an hour."

"Fine," she said. "Then we'll see you at ten o'clock. Good-bye."

Perky, Harry thought gloomily as he swung out of bed, perky as the receptionist in a dentist's office. Just the type of girl Rothko would hire.

William T. Rothko was known as an up-and-coming young man. Barely thirty-five years old, he had given up a lucrative law practice to run for district attorney, winning the office by a landslide vote. Tall, lean, personable, he was a campaign manager's joy, but underneath his boyish good looks there was a core of spring steel. That core was evident as he rose from behind his desk and greeted Harry with marked coolness.

"Inspector. Take a seat."

104

There was another man in Rothko's oak-paneled office, a stout, gray-haired man who wore pince-nez glasses on the tip of his nose. He was seated in a far corner of the room, his lips moving soundlessly as he scanned some papers in his hands. He seemed oblivious to Harry's presence.

Rothko sat back in his chair and shuffled through a document lying open on his desk.

"I've been looking over your arrest report, Callahan. A very unusual piece of police work. Really amazing."

"I had some luck."

Rothko looked up sharply. "Is that what you call it, luck? The only *luck,* Callahan, is that this office isn't indicting you for assault with intent to commit murder!"

Harry stiffened as though slapped in the face. "What are you talking about?"

Rothko picked up the document and waved it at Harry. *"This.* Who the hell gave you the right to kick down doors, torture suspects, deny medical attention and legal counsel? Where have you been for the past five years? Doesn't Escobedo ring a bell? Miranda? Surely you must have heard of the fourth amendment? What I'm saying to you is that man had rights."

"Yeah. I'm all broken up about his rights." Harry's tone was defensive. He felt confused, unsure of his position or why he was being attacked.

"You should be broken up," Rothko said sharply. "I've got a little news for you. As soon as the suspect's well enough to leave the hospital, he *walks.*"

Anger rose in Harry. "What are you handing me, Rothko?"

"The facts of life, Callahan. He goes free. We can't go before the grand jury because we don't have one shred of evidence."

Harry jumped to his feet. "Evidence? What the hell do you need? Have you seen the rifle? The machine pistol?"

"I've seen them," Rothko replied dryly. "They're
105

nice looking weapons, but they aren't worth a damn to me."

"Are you trying to tell me that Ballistics can't match up the bullets we dug out of Sandra Benson and the Russell kid with that hunting rifle?"

"No, I'm not saying that at all. The bullets do match, but the rifle is inadmissible as evidence and there are no prints on the machine pistol . . . nothing to tie it in with the suspect. There were two clips of nine-millimeter bullets in the bottom of the suitcase, but that's inadmissible too. I don't have a case, Callahan, I have a house of cards. I don't have one scrap of real evidence against this man. *Nothing.*"

"Who the hell says so?" Harry was shouting now and his face was the color of weathered brick.

"The law!" Rothko shouted back.

"Then the law's crazy!"

The two men were glowering at one another like two bulldogs.

The elderly man in the corner of the room rose majestically from his chair. "I can understand your confusion, Mr. Callahan. Perhaps if I explained."

Harry looked at him with a who-the-hell-are-you expression written all over his face. Rothko caught it and moved quickly to avoid further unpleasantness.

"Callahan, let me introduce Judge Bannerman of the appellate court. He also meets classes in constitutional law at Berkeley. I asked him to come in because I value his opinion. I would like you to listen to him."

"I'll listen," Harry muttered.

Judge Bannerman slipped off his glasses and tucked them in his breast pocket. "This is obiter dictum of course. But in my opinion the search of the suspect's quarters was illegal and any evidence obtained thereby —that hunting rifle, for instance—is inadmissible in court. You should have taken the time to get a search warrant, inspector. I'm sorry, but it's that simple."

"A girl was dying." Harry's voice was strained.

"She was already dead," Rothko said evenly.

"I didn't know that at the time. As far as I knew I was fighting a clock . . . a deadline."

Judge Bannerman nodded in agreement. "The court would certainly take into recognition your legitimate concern for the girl's life, but in no way could they possibly condone the use of police torture to extract what amounted to an admission of guilt. No, Mr. Callahan, the suspect's confession and all physical evidence would have to be excluded. The suspect's rights were clearly violated under the fourth, fifth, and probably the sixth and fourteenth amendments."

Harry felt suddenly very cold. When he spoke, his voice came from a great distance. "What about Mary Ann Deacon's rights? She was tortured, raped, and jammed into a box to die. Who speaks for her? What amendment does she fall under?"

"The law may not always seem fair," Judge Bannerman said kindly. "But it must always be just. It cannot be twisted to fit all circumstances—no matter how appalling those circumstances might be."

Rothko looked anguished. "Callahan. For Christ's sake, do you think I enjoy letting this guy off the hook? I've got a wife and two little girls. I don't want him on the streets any more than you do—or Judge Bannerman. But facts remain facts. I *can't get an indictment.*"

"So it was all for nothing." Harry's voice was toneless.

"Nothing."

"He won't be on the streets for long."

Rothko's eyebrows quivered. "What does that mean?"

"He'll stub his toes. And I'll be there when he does."

"This office won't tolerate harassment. Let's get that clear right now."

Harry compressed his lips into a bloodless line. "You haven't heard the last of this guy. He's going to keep on killing people."

"How do you know that?"

Harry looked at the district attorney in surprise, as though the reason was so obvious it hardly required an explanation. "Because he likes it, Rothko. He really and truly likes it."

VIII

Women sense the force of my sensuality. It intrigues and excites them. Scorpios are sexual people . . . they satisfy women. Women know this . . . they can tell. It's an instinct.

"Hello," he said. "Would you like to go home with me?"

The girl ignored him. She flounced on past the bar, her buttocks moving loosely under thin, scarlet panties, her breasts bare, powdered, the thick nipples heavily rouged. Her breasts swayed and bounced as she walked.

"Bitch," the man said into the froth of his beer.

He drank slowly, making it last. On a raised dais behind the bar, a girl writhed on a bed. She was totally naked, her flesh mauve under the colored spotlight . . . mauve, then . . . green . . . orange. Her nipples appeared black under the lights. She scissored her legs invitingly and made love to the edge of the mattress.

"Bitch."

He felt hot and uncomfortable. The tiny North Beach bar was jammed with men. They pressed up against him and reached over his shoulder for their glasses of beer. They blew cigarette smoke in his face and he could hear their obscene talk.

Bastards.

He drained his glass and pushed through the crowd toward the door. Out of the corner of his eye, he could see a man get up from a table and follow after him—a tall, lean man dressed in gray slacks and a leather windbreaker.

The son of a bitch!

He trembled with suppressed rage as he limped out of the bar and into the crowd moving along Greenwich. He knew that he was right behind him, keeping an even distance . . . never closer . . . never farther away . . . always steadily behind him, going where he went, watching him. He crossed Greenwich against the traffic and cursed himself for having allowed Harry Francis Callahan to live. That had been a great mistake. He had toyed with the bastard. He shouldn't have done that. He should have said nothing to him, not a word. He should have been waiting in the ferns by the cross, and when Harry Francis Callahan arrived, he should have pumped a clip of shells into him. He should have split him open like a watermelon.

Pig!

He ducked into an alley, but before he was halfway down it he could hear footsteps coming after him. Callahan was hard to shake. He had been trying for over a week, ever since he had left the hospital. Every night it had been the same. No matter what he did or where he went Callahan would be trailing him like the tail on a kite.

He stopped at a juice stand and bought an orange drink. It was eleven fifteen and he had committed himself to a course of action that would settle the problem of Harry Francis Callahan once and for all—not the solution he would have preferred, but *smarter*. Scorpios were subtle people.

He strolled down the street, jostled by the Saturday night crowd. He paused in front of a movie theater and studied the photographs on the display board. Naked couples sprawled on oval beds, their genitals discreetly covered by strips of black tape.

FREEDOM TO LOVE!
SWEDISH INNOCENCE IN ALL ITS GRAPHIC BEAUTY.
SUPREME COURT RULING BENEFITS YOU.

He gave the cashier a five-dollar bill and went inside.
He crossed the lobby and took the left-hand door into
the theater. The picture was playing but he didn't bother
to glance at the screen. He hurried across the empty
top row, waited a moment at the right-hand door, and
then went back into the lobby. He could see a flash of
gray slacks and brown leather jacket go in through the
opposite door and he grinned to himself. He was still
grinning when he hailed a cab in front of the theater and
climbed quickly inside.

He paid the driver off at Cathay Basin. The driver
looked uneasily at the dark, deserted street, the rows of
rotting abandoned warehouses.

"Are you sure you wanna get out here, mister?"

"I have to meet somebody . . . a Mr. Harry Callahan.
He told me to meet him at the corner of Cathay Basin
and Berry Street."

"Well, that's where we are, but it's a hell of a place
to pick. You want me to wait around in case he don't
show?"

"Oh, he'll show. He works for the police department.
He's always punctual."

"Suit yourself, buddy."

He waited on the corner until the cab made a U-turn
and drove off at high speed. When its red taillights faded
in the distance, he walked quickly down the center of
the street until he came abreast of a warehouse that bore
the faded legend Philippine Pacific Lines across the corrugated iron front. A small, tin-sheathed door was ajar,
creaking slowly on rusted hinges. He went inside, step-
ping into musty darkness.

"It's about time. I was goin' to split." The voice was
deep, as though it came from the bottom of a pit. A
black man stood in the center of the warehouse floor.

Slivers of moonlight filtered down on him from dust-caked windows high in the roof. The pale light revealed nothing about him other than his size. He was smaller than a barn door, but only just.

"I had to ditch him."

"Callahan? Don't kid me."

"I'm here, aren't I?"

The black man only grunted. "How much did you bring?"

"Two hundred."

The black man whistled softly. "You really want that much, baby?"

"Every penny of it."

"You're something else. I gotta say that for you."

"I'm not interested in your opinion of me. Take the money and get on with it."

"Anything you say, baby. It's your party." He held out a big hand. "Lay it on me, baby."

He walked up to the man and placed four fifty-dollar bills in his palm. The man held each bill up to the meager light, grunted his satisfaction, and shoved the bills into his pocket.

"Two bills' worth coming up, baby. See that crate over there? Go sit on it. Might as well be comfortable. Right? No point in floppin' all over the motherin' floor."

He walked over to the crate and sat down. His eyes were tiny pinpoints of blue as he watched the black man take a pair of leather gloves from his belt and put them on with loving care, finger by finger, smoothing them, flexing his thick-fingered hands.

"You are really somethin' else, baby," the black man said. "You're one for the motherin' book."

"Shut up," he hissed. "You've got your fuckin' money. Get on with it."

The black man bowed deeply and moved toward the crate, toward the stiffly seated figure. He came at a slow shuffle, his feet scraping on the concrete floor. "I'sa comin' Massa Jack . . . I'sa comin', an' ma haid is bendin' low . . ." His right arm moved back cocked like the

112

hammer on a gun. Then it exploded, moving straight out from the shoulder, the tight leather wad of his fist slamming like a trip hammer on the slim white nose before him. There was the nasty crack of bone as the pale blob of a face snapped to one side, spraying blood.

He did not make a sound.

"Mother," the black man whispered.

"Get on with it, you black son of a bitch!"

"OK, baby. You're *the* man."

He hit him and kept on hitting him, with an almost surgical precision, measuring his blows, timing the short lefts and rights so that the man on the crate simply rocked from side to side and never fell off. Only once did his timing fail him. He hit the man's jaw with a long, looping right and forgot to counter with his left. The man spun off the crate and fell heavily to the floor. He reached down and plucked him up like a rag doll, placing him back on his perch.

"How ya doin', baby?"

The man muttered something, but his words were lost as they bubbled up through a mouth full of blood. The black man took a deep breath and swung up from the floor. His blood-soaked leather fist sounded like the slap of a wet towel as it thudded home. Then he stepped back as the seated figure doubled over and pitched forward to sprawl at his feet.

"Is that enough, boy?" The black man was breathing heavily and a river of sweat had plastered his shirt to his body. He was 285 pounds and not all of it was muscle.

"Go . . . screw . . ."

The black man sighed. "Two hundred the man said. Two hundred it is." He kicked the twisted figure in the ribs, again and again. It was a challenge—his shoe versus the man's bones. He kicked to win.

The scream sliced through the warehouse, jangling the nerves like an electric shock. The black man stepped away from the writhing, contorted creature on the floor and peeled off his soggy gloves.

DIRTY HARRY

"Two bills . . . right to the last dime." He bent down with a sigh, picked up his customer, and carried him to the door. "It's been a pleasure," he said as he tossed the bloody bundle into the middle of the street. "You ofay bastard."

The press, always loath to see a good story die, latched on to the incident the moment reporters covering San Francisco General Hospital phoned in the report. Files were hurriedly brought up from the morgues of every newspaper.

IS THIS MAN "SCORPIO"?
DID HE OR DIDN'T HE?—DO THE POLICE
KNOW FOR SURE?
WHO IS THIS MAN?

He gives no name. Who is this nameless wanderer, this pathetic semirecluse?

NO PRINTS ON RECORD, D. A. SAYS

William T. Rothko admitted today that an exhaustive search of FBI fingerprint files failed to . . .

NO CASE, ROTHKO ADMITS
SOLON ADVISES POLICE CLEANUP

Certain peculiarities in police procedure have sparked State Senator Alvin W. . . .

"Get on to it, Bert," the city editor of the *Post-Advocate* advised his best feature writer. "The ambulance men who picked him up say he kept mumbling that a cop beat him up. Something smells. Find out where the stink's coming from."

The morning sun struck the tall windows of the corridor. The sun and the portable lights held by the TV crews served to broil everyone unfortunate enough to

114

be packed into the narrow space between the elevator and the office of Dennis J. Cooper, M.D., chief resident. Dr. Cooper came out of his office and glared owlishly into the sun and the lights.

"I have no statement to make at this time."

"Please, doctor, just one question. Would you say that this man had sustained a beating?"

"He has multiple facial fractures and six fractured ribs, two of them compound. I can only say that he was badly injured. By what or by whom I could not, with any authority, say."

"Will you permit him to speak with the press?"

"Not at this time. His jaws have just been wired. No. I cannot permit him to speak to anyone."

"When can he do so?"

"Gentlemen, I'm sorry. I'm a busy man. I don't wish to make a statement at this time. Let me through, please . . . let me through."

"Keep on it, Bert. Sit on his doorstep. Something smells. Something stinks."

The newsmen waited till noon and then were granted permission to conduct a brief interview with the victim on a pool basis—one TV cameraman and one newspaper reporter covering the story for all.

He was heavily bandaged. What the newsmen could see of his face was bloated and grotesque. His lips were thick, liver-colored slabs and he moved them with great difficulty. The reporter sat by the side of his bed and the cameraman set up his Beaulieu near the door so that he could include the interviewer in the shot. Both men were hushed, awed, as though attending the last rites.

"There is a rumor that you are claiming police harassment and brutality, that the San Francisco Police Department did this to you. Is that correct, sir?"

The man moved his lips slowly. His speech was blurred, difficult to hear. "I swear it. As God is my judge."

"But, why would they do that? What purpose could they have?"

"I . . . don't know. Tried . . . to frame me . . . Deacon case. Now, trying to kill me. Cops . . . follow me . . . everywhere . . . hound me . . . beat me."

"Did you get a look at the man who did this to you?"

"Yes. Met me . . . in a movie . . . on Stockton . . . told me . . . meet him later at warehouse . . . very important."

"And you went?"

"Trusted him. I . . . was . . . sucker."

"And who was this man?"

"Detective . . . Homicide . . . big guy . . . name of Callahan."

There was another man in San Francisco General Hospital that bright and sunny day in whom the newspapermen had no interest. Chico Gonsales, his tall, muscular body looking fit and trim in gym shorts and T-shirt, stood in the physical therapy room struggling to raise his left arm higher than his nose. He didn't make it, but he came close.

"That was good, Chico. That was *very* good," the therapist purred. She was young, pretty, and black and she moved with the easy grace of a tennis player. "I want you to squeeze the rubber ball for fifteen minutes and then we'll have half an hour in the whirlpool. OK?"

"OK," Chico said dully. "Anything you say."

Norma Gonsales, pert, blonde, and eight months pregnant, sat in a far corner of the bright, pleasant room knitting a baby sweater and chatting with Harry Callahan.

"He's coming along great," Harry lied.

Norma shook her head. "He could try harder. Being like that . . . well, he was always such an active man."

"It takes time."

"He's not very patient, I guess." She bent over her

116

knitting for a moment and then said, quietly and evenly, "He's going to quit."

"Tell him to sleep on it. He's a good man and I like him."

She glanced up at Harry, her face grave. "So do I, Mr. Callahan. It's my fault that he's leaving. I thought I could take it but I don't have the class."

"Don't run yourself down."

She shook her head sharply. "No. Whatever it takes to be a cop's wife, I haven't got it. He has teaching credentials. I want him to teach in some nice, quiet high school. I can't watch him leave the house every day and wonder if I'll ever see him alive again. I don't know . . . am I wrong? Am I the only one who feels like that? Doesn't it drive your wife crazy?"

"It did, at one time."

"You mean, she got used to it?"

"She was killed in a car accident before she had a chance to find out. We hadn't been married very long."

She looked away, dropping her eyes to the ball of powder blue wool in her lap. "I'm sorry."

"That's OK. It was a long, long time ago." He glanced at his watch. "Well, I better get downtown. Tell Chico for me that he's doing the right thing. He has my blessing. It's no life."

She smiled, relieved and grateful. "Why do you stay in it, Mr. Callahan?"

Harry made a vague gesture. "I don't know. I really don't know."

The evening editions and the four o'clock television news came out at the same time. The effect of the dual coverage set telephones to jangling from one end of City Hall to the other. When the storm hit, Harry Callahan was sharing a hero sandwich with Frank Di Georgio in the inspectors' lounge. The crisp voice over the PA system bore not a hint of censure as it asked him to report to the chief's office.

It was muggy in the chief's office and Harry unbuttoned his coat before sitting down. The chief scrutinized him, his pale blue eyes flinty hard.

"What do you do with your free time, Harry?"

Harry met the chief's gaze unflinchingly. "I've been tailing the Deacon case suspect."

"*Ex*-suspect, Harry."

"OK . . . I've been tailing the ex-suspect in the Deacon case."

"Do you know what happened to him last night?"

"I heard a rumor over the grapevine that someone beat him up."

"He claims you did."

"He can claim anything he wants, but I never laid a finger on him."

"Did you see him last night? Did he see you?"

"Yes. He saw me. I lost him in a porno movie house on Stockton. The cashier said she saw him come out a moment after I went in. He grabbed a cab."

The chief tapped the edge of his desk with a pencil. "That's right, Harry. He took a taxi to Cathay Basin and Berry Street. According to the evening paper, the driver of that taxi remembers the man telling him he was going there to meet a police officer . . . named Callahan. Did you meet him, Harry?"

"No. I told you, he gave me the slip."

The pencil went tap-tap-tap. "Rothko's furious . . . so is the mayor."

"Do they really believe I slapped the guy around?"

"No . . . I don't think they believe it. The press is playing it up, but there's a lot of politics involved. You know, two months before election day. What really bothers the DA is the harassment charge. You've been tailing the guy. You can't deny that."

"I wouldn't even try."

"Did Bressler OK it?"

"I don't ask the lieutenant what to do on my off hours."

The chief pursed his lips and swung sideways in his

chair. "I thought it was something like that. Just Harry Callahan doing his own little thing."

"Do you want my star?"

"No. That wouldn't do anybody any good. All I want is for you to put an end to this . . . surveillance of an innocent man."

Harry snorted. "That's just what he's after."

The chief swung back to the desk and tossed his pencil down on the blotter. "What makes you think that?"

"Because he's going to kill again. I can sense it, chief. He's tight as a spring. He's going to kill again. The only question is who . . . where . . . and how."

IX

*The stars impel but do not compel. That's fact . . .
that's logic. The stars direct all of our destinies . . . mine
and his. If our stars cross up there in the blackness,
that's the way it is. I have no control over that. That's
fate. Our lives are mixed up in the stars . . . my life
. . . his life . . . all of our lives. Mixed in Capricorn . . .
Libra . . . Leo . . . Scorpio. Crossed in the stars . . .
Mine . . . his . . .*

He stood bareheaded in the light rain and examined
the bottles so neatly displayed in the store window A
woman walked out of the store carrying two quart
bottles of soda in a paper sack and a bottle of sherry
that she had wedged into her handbag. After she had
gone, the store was empty of customers and the street
lay deserted except for a car moving up it, its tires
humming on the wet asphalt.

He turned up his coat collar and went into the store,
moving hesitantly past the shelves of liquor bottles. The
man behind the counter looked up from a racing form
and watched him. He was a big man, soft and flabby,
with tiny, suspicious eyes.

"What can I do you for, Jack?"

"Well, I'm not sure." He moved up to the counter
and peered intently at the rows of bottles. His eyes were

120

sunk deeply in puffy flesh and his nose and lips were crisscrossed with tiny black holes where the stitches had been. "I'm not sure what I want."

"Take your time." The proprietor couldn't keep his eyes off the wrecked face. "If you don't mind my askin', what the hell happened to you, Jack?"

He smiled bleakly. "I lost a fight in Denver. I'm a fighter . . . welterweight. I had a real bad night."

"I can see that. What happened, he hit you with the stool?"

"He was tough. A Mexican kid. Mexicans are real tough."

"That one sure and hell was. Christ." He shuddered slightly and looked away. "Well, just take your time lookin'. If I can help you, just sing out."

"I'll do that. You see . . . being a fighter, I don't drink. I've never had a drink in my life. I've been invited to a party and I want to bring something nice. Something good. You know . . . something around nine . . . ten bucks."

The proprietor perked up. "How about a bottle of French cognac? Imported from France. Only eight bucks and a hell of a nice gift. Fancy, you know . . . make a good impression."

"Fine. I'll take it."

The proprietor took a bottle of cognac from one of the lower shelves and placed it on the counter. "Remy-Martin. A fine brand. You want I should wrap it? I got some nice paper."

"No, that's OK." He toyed with a box of Chiclets lying open in front of the cash register and watched the man put the bottle in a bag. "Isn't this the store I read about, the one that's been robbed so many times?"

The proprietor smiled grimly. "That's right, Jack. Fourteen times in three years. Last two times I sent 'em out of here on platters. I'm getting to be a pretty good shot and I keep the baby handy." He set the bottle down and lifted the front edge of his sweater. The ugly black handle of a Luger stuck up from the waistband of his pants, jutting over the swell of his belly.

"I can draw the damn thing faster than Matt Di—" He never got the name out. The man across the counter backhanded him across the mouth with the bottle in the bag. He staggered back, bleeding, not believing it was happening. "No . . ." he tried to scream, but the bottle hit him again, across the cheek, not breaking, thudding into him hard and stunning—a glass club. He fell heavily in the narrow space between the counter and the shelves, whipped by pain and terror.

"Take it . . . take the money . . . take it."

"Fuck the money," the man said, standing over him, smiling at him through scarred lips. He reached down and took the gun, balanced it in his hand for a moment and then jammed it under his belt.

"Where do you keep the extra shells?"

"Shells?" The proprietor was bewildered. "Shells?"

The man kicked him in the head, just behind the ear. "Bullets! you fat clod—*bullets*. Where do you keep them?"

"Under the counter. Don't kill me—please don't kill me."

"Kill you?" he said. "That's a dumb thing to say. Why would I want to kill you?"

Someplace there would be stars. A wilderness of stars. Stars and no people. Stars and no buildings . . . no lights. Nothing but sky. Where? Africa? Asia? Where?

"Deep in the heart of Texas," he said. A man seated next to him on the crosstown bus looked at him oddly and changed his seat.

Well, that was a goddamn lie because he had been in Dallas and there had been nothing but buildings and a yellow haze hanging over the city in the heat. At night there had been a hard, sandy wind and nothing in the sky but grit. *Someplace.* But where?

"Do you have the time, lady?" He leaned across the

aisle, startling a woman who had just sat down, her arms filled with groceries.

"I . . . I don't know . . . about noon, I guess." She was staring at his face.

"Thank you." He smiled wanly. "I was in a motorcycle accident. My brother got killed."

"Oh, my . . . I'm so sorry."

"That's OK."

The old bitch.

Noon. And the stars up there where you couldn't see them. The sun burning them out. But up there . . . waiting for night to fall. Night was coming early. It was coming early for lots of people.

He left the bus at the corner of Noriega and Sixteenth Avenue and walked up the hill toward Fifteenth. The rain had stopped and the sun was turning the wet pavement to steam. It was tiring going up the hill and he did not press himself. He could tell by the small group of women waiting at the corner that he had plenty of time. When he joined them, he leaned back against a retaining wall to catch his breath. The women chatted idly among themselves and one or two of them glanced in his direction. It was nearly twelve thirty when a small, yellow school bus ground its way down Fifteenth from Lawton and pulled up at the corner. There were a dozen first- and second-graders in the bus, all of them screaming and bouncing around on the seats. When the doors opened, about half of them piled out, going through the door two abreast, pushing and shoving for the honor of being first out of the bus.

"Davey! Don't shove Miriam like that!"

"Mama! Can I have a taco for lunch?"

"Can Mary stay over, can she? Can she?"

Words spilled over one another in a cacophony of shrill sounds. Then the women and children were gone, scattering off in all directions like startled birds.

He stepped into the bus before the driver could close the door. An elderly woman, her large body encased in baggy blue slacks and an Eisenhower jacket, a peaked cap pinned precariously to a mass of tight, brassy curls, she looked at the man in startled confusion.

"Hey, you can't come inside, mister."

"City bus inspector, lady." He beamed a smile on the children who had stopped shouting at each other long enough to stare at this unusual intrusion. "Hiya there, kids!"

Six kids shouted the greeting back at him and one, for no apparent reason, burst into tears.

"Bus inspector?" The driver was filled with doubt. "I never heard of a bus inspector coming on a bus in the middle of a route. I got a schedule, mister, an' I gotta keep it."

He pressed up against her side, drawing the Luger from his belt and poking the hard, cold barrel into one sagging breast. "Shut up, you silly old bitch. Get moving or I'll blow your flabby body all over this bus."

She was a big, formidable woman. A no-nonsense woman. She wasn't the kind of woman who took any gaff from anybody, but when she looked hard into this man's face, she could see only death.

"All right," she whispered. "Where do you want to go?"

"Just drive. I'll tell you what to do. Drive nice and easy. Try anything funny and you'll have a busload of dead kids."

"Don't frighten them. Please. Don't frighten them."

"It's up to you, lady." He sprawled out on the empty front seat, the Luger concealed by his jacket. "Any of you kids know a song?"

They all shouted a name at the same time.

" 'Old MacDonald,' " he shouted back. "I know that one." He started to sing, his voice hard, strident, drowning out the grinding mesh of the gears as the bus lurched forward.

" 'Old MacDonald had a farm, eeyi, eeyi, oh . . . And on that farm he had some chicks, eeyi, eeyi, oh . . .' "

It had started out as a good day for Harry Callahan. The telephone had rung the moment he had come into the office at eight thirty. The caller had been the desk sergeant at Park Station, the center of the Haight-Ashbury district. The night watch had brought in somebody that maybe Harry would be interested in talking to—a big, red-headed kid who had been picked up for purse snatching in Golden Gate Park.

"Our Buena Vista mugger!" Harry had shouted at Di Georgio as he went toward the door. "No wonder he hasn't been around lately—he switched to purses!"

It had been him all right, but it had taken Harry till noon to make him admit it. Finally he cracked, sobbing, sorry as hell that he had hit one of the old men hard enough to kill him. Harry was sorry too, but that's how it went. He booked him on a charge of murder.

He was having a cup of coffee with one of the Park Station detectives when he got a call from Lieutenant Bressler. Bressler's voice was muffled, as though he were speaking with his mouth pressed against the phone.

"You wrap it up, Harry?"

"Oh, sure. He cracked wide open."

"Good . . . good. Listen, Harry . . . the mayor wants to see you. Right away."

"The mayor wants to see *me?*"

"On the double, Harry. I . . . I'll meet you in the rotunda . . . clue you in when you get there. Snap it up."

Harry drove to the Civic Center mall with the siren wailing. He parked in a red zone and walked briskly into City Hall. Bressler met him in the rotunda, looking out of place amid the marble stairs and balustrades. He looked worried and decidedly uncomfortable.

"What's happening, Al?"

"It's Scorpio again, Harry."

Harry kept his face straight, not a flicker of an I-told-you-so expression. "What did he do this time?"

"We don't know yet. That's the trouble. The mayor got a note from him. It came special delivery at nine

125

o'clock this morning. He'll read it to you, but I wanted to talk to you first." He paused with one foot on the broad marble stairs. "I want you to do what he asks, Harry. I want you to play this one the mayor's way . . . straight down the middle."

Harry only grunted. It could have meant anything.

They mounted the broad stairs side by side and in silence. Then Bressler said, "I got a long report from the Springfield, Massachusetts, police this morning. They think our Scorpio is Charles Davis . . . an escaped mental patient. He was committed when he was fourteen for killing his parents and a younger sister with a shotgun. He escaped five years later and hasn't been heard of since. That was a long time ago, but they feel he's our boy."

"So he has a name," Harry said dourly. "So what?"

"So nothing," Bressler snapped. "I thought you might be interested."

"I'm only interested in what his honor has to say." He went up the stairs two at a time and Bressler had to hustle to keep up with him.

The mayor greeted Harry crisply but cordially. He was not a man to harbor grudges even if he never forgot a slight or a bad turn. The electorate had given him the city for another four years by the biggest vote margin in the city's history and he led Harry through his suite of offices like a man comfortably at home. There seemed to be a hell of a lot of activity. Every phone was manned and four of the mayor's aides were seated at a long table in the conference room counting out stacks of twenty-dollar bills.

"What's going on, Mr. Mayor?"

The mayor pressed his fingers into Harry's arm and ushered him into his private office. He waited for Bressler to join them and then shut the door.

"I received a note from Scorpio. It came early this morning. It may or may not be a hoax. We just have to sweat it out."

126

"Can I read it?"

The mayor crossed to his desk, picked up a sheet of paper and handed it to him. The note was like the last one—hand written, each letter copybook perfect.

TO THE CITY OF SAN FRANCISCO:
GREETINGS. YOU BASTARDS HAVE DOUBLE-CROSSED ME FOR THE LAST TIME. I AM WARNING YOU. I WANT MY TWO HUNDRED THOUSAND DOLLARS. I WANT A JET PLANE READY AND WAITING. I WILL CALL THE MAYOR AT ONE O'CLOCK THIS AFTERNOON AND TELL HIM ABOUT HOSTAGES I HOLD AND WHO I WILL BE HAPPY TO KILL. DON'T BLOW THIS ONE.

SCORPIO

Harry handed the note back. "It's ten after one now."

The mayor's face was grave. "It's too early to relax. As I said, it may be a false alarm—a little joke—but I can't chance it. I have the money . . . it's being counted now . . . and I have a 707 waiting out at Santa Rosa airport, fueled and ready to go."

Harry's grin was sardonic. "You've thought of everything. What do you need me for?"

The mayor hesitated for a fraction of a second, then turned back to his desk. "There was a postscript . . . on a separate sheet of paper." He picked it up and held it out to Harry, who did not have to take it from the mayor's hand to see what was scrawled across it.

CALLAHAN DELIVERS!

A woman's voice over the intercom system broke the uncomfortable silence in the room.

"Mr. Mayor, there's a call for you on line two."

The mayor moved rapidly to his desk and switched on the conference phone. "This is the mayor speaking."

They could hear traffic sounds, the swoosh and whine of cars moving at high speed. Near a freeway, Harry mused. He recognized the killer's voice as soon as he spoke.

"Greetings, mayor. I've got somebody in the booth with me I'd like you to talk to. One of your bus drivers, mayor. I've got seven kids from the Lawton Street school . . . cute little tykes, mayor. Real cute bunch of kids. I've got the bus driver and I've got the bus. What do you think of that?"

"Now you listen to me for a minute, Scorpio . . ."

"No. You listen to me. You listen to the driver. Tell him . . . go on, tell him."

A woman's voice came over the line, thin, quavering. "It wasn't my fault . . . he has a gun."

"Tell him your name, bitch!"

"Platt . . . Mrs. Marcella Platt. I'm sorry, Mr. Mayor, I'm . . ."

"That's all right," the mayor said.

The killer chuckled. "You don't have to bother checking the broad out. You know me. I don't bullshit anybody. I've got the kids, and if you start screwing me around, they start dying . . . one by one. Is the plane ready?"

Harry leaned toward the mayor and mouthed the words: *Stall him.*

The mayor shook his head quickly. "There is a 707 jet being fueled right now at Santa Rosa Municipal Airport. The money will be there by the time you arrive."

"Stall him," Harry said silently.

"Be smart this time," the killer warned. "We're just going to be driving along nice and easy. A bus full of kids. I don't want to see any cop cars. I don't want to see any helicopters. You play it square with me and the kids'll have a nice little ride. OK?"

The mayor avoided Harry's eyes. "OK. I guarantee that you won't be molested in any way. You have my word of honor on this."

There was a sharp clicking sound and then the hum

of the dial tone. The mayor switched off the instrument. "You all heard him."

"You have to stop this guy," Harry said.

A vein bulged in the mayor's forehead. "If we make any move to stop him, he's going to start killing children."

"He's going to start killing children anyway—just to show his contempt for us. And me . . . what the hell do you think he has in store for me after I hand him the money? You think he's going to shake my hand and thank me?"

"That's a risk, of course."

"Sure—well, I'll take any risk in the world, but not with my hands tied behind my back."

The vein bulged out like a piece of blue rope. "He will not be molested in any way. I gave my word and I intend to keep it. That's a direct order, Callahan."

"Fine. Good. Swell. But you can get yourself another delivery boy." He swung on his heels and stormed out of the office, startling the secretaries in the outer office by the fury of his stride.

He drove north, over the graceful span of the Golden Gate Bridge and into the lush countryside of Marin County. He caught up with the school bus on the freeway three miles past Novato, roaring by it on the far lane, sitting hunched down behind the wheel. He caught a brief glimpse of the killer standing in the front of the bus, facing the children. His arms were moving up and down as though conducting an orchestra. Harry wondered what the man was up to as he pulled far ahead of the bus and eased over to the right-hand lane.

" 'Row row row your boat gently down the stream . . . Merrily merrily merrily merrily life is but a dream . . .' "

He was singing alone. The children sat in their seats, staring at him. They were tired, hungry, and confused.

"I wanna go home!" a little girl wailed.

The killer forced a grin. "We're going to the ice

129

cream factory. Don't you want to go to the ice cream factory too?"

"No!" the child cried. "I wanna go home!"

"So do I!" A boy jumped up and ran down the aisle toward the front of the bus. He had a baseball mitt on one hand and a book clutched in the other. "I wanna go home too."

The killer slapped him hard across the face and shoved him into the front seat. The sound of the slap sounded loud in the cavernous, nearly empty bus. The boy glared at him, his face red as he struggled to hold back the tears.

Mrs. Platt bristled. "You shouldn't have done that!"

"Shut up," he said harshly. "Just drive the goddamn bus."

They were twenty-three miles from Santa Rosa.

Harry took the airport turnoff and made a sharp right at the bottom of the ramp. He drove slowly for two miles along Drake Boulevard until he reached the Southern Pacific railway trestle. The Southern Pacific spur line flanked the west end of the airport and then cut over the highway on a low, wooden trestle that was already tagged for demolition and replacement. He pulled off the road behind the trestle, took off his jacket, made doubly sure that the big Smith and Wesson was secure in the shoulder holster and then left the car and climbed up the embankment.

DANGER—KEEP OFF
S.P.R.R.

The small metal sign was nailed to a post, the lettering on it badly peppered by generations of BB gun shooters. Harry barely glanced at it as he started across the trestle, keeping to the outside edge. The heavy timbers stank of creosote and the shiny rails gleamed in the sun. He made his way to the center of the span and swung his legs over the guard railing and sat down on a beam, his back to the railing and his legs dangling in space. North-bound traffic moved fourteen feet eight inches below him in a slow, steady stream.

The bus was locked in the traffic stream just as Harry had figured it would be at this time of the afternoon. He could see it coming from a long way off, the yellow paint and the black lettering standing out clearly. He waited for it, his body tense, his hands gripping the edge of the protruding wooden beam.

Jesus! The traffic wasn't moving fast but it wasn't stalled either, and the closer the bus came the faster it seemed to be going. What he was about to do wasn't something that one had the time to give a great deal of thought to. It was something that had to be done quickly or not done at all. He saw the killer's white startled face stare up at him through the windshield and then he was off, pushing away with his hands, falling feet first into space. He hit the roof of the bus ten feet from the front and sprawled heavily on hands and knees, sliding toward the rear with sickening speed. He dropped flat and clawed desperately at the metal luggage skids that ran the length of the roof, tearing his fingernails to shreds, but stopping what would have been a one-way slide to death. The fall had jammed the butt of the magnum into his collarbone and pain ripped him from neck to waist.

"You son of a bitch." The killer's scream turned the children into cowering animals, huddling against a terror they could not fathom. They clung to one another and slid to the floor of the bus behind the screen of the seats. Mrs. Marcella Platt held onto the wheel with leaden hands, closed her eyes, and shrieked her head off. The bus drifted toward the other side of the road. The killer spun toward her, gripped her by the hair, and yanked her off her seat. She sprawled on the floorboards, her head down in the well of the front door, still screaming as though she never would stop—not in this life.

He was behind the wheel now, steering the bus with

131

one hand, straddling the center line, oblivious to the howl of car horns. He jammed the pedal to the floor and pressed a hand over the horn button, scattering the traffic ahead of him, forcing room.

"Bastard . . . stinking pig."

He tugged the Luger out of his belt, half turned in his seat and sent four shots up through different sections of the roof.

The bullets ripped through the thin steel in front of and behind Harry. There was no question of trying to get out of the way of any more shots, there was nowhere to go. He lay spread-eagled face downward, his fingers clawed on the chrome runners. The bus rocked from side to side, yawing badly as the killer yanked the wheel from right to left, trying to throw him off.

Two more shots tore upward, off center this time, punching neat holes near the join of the roof six inches from Harry's right hand.

He was still up there, but he had a tiger by the tail.

If only they'd stop screaming. Why do they have to keep on screaming? I'm not doing anything to them . . . nothing. Why can't they shut up? Why do they keep on screaming like that?

He glanced over his shoulder. He couldn't see any of the children, but their voices rose in one continuous howl of blind terror.

"Shut up, goddamn it . . . shut up."

But the screaming grew louder. He waved the Luger, then leveled it at the head of Mrs. Marcella Platt: "Tell the bastards to shut up! Tell them."

Mrs. Platt only screamed. It was a chain link fence that kept a bullet from splitting her brain.

The bus had drifted to the left-hand side of the road, heading toward the mile-long fence that marked the boundary of the Murchison Gravel Works. The killer saw the fence a second before he plowed into it. He jammed the wheel hard to the right and the bus skidded on the shoulder of the road and lurched heavily to one side, sideswiping the fence with a hideous screech of metal against metal. The steel mesh parted, torn to shreds by the momentum and weight of the big vehicle. The killer struggled with the wheel to get back onto the road, but the tires slid on the soft dirt and the bus careened into the plant yard and plowed to a stop against a mountain of gravel.

Harry flew forward, his fingers clutching nothing but swirling clouds of dust. He landed on his side and felt himself sinking into a choking river of reddish sand. He was drowning in it and he clawed his way free, rolling to the hard ground in a billow of dust that left him gasping for breath. He dug sand and gravel out of his eyes and staggered to his feet. The bus was ten yards from him, half buried in the pile with its rear door open. Drawing his revolver, he ran toward it and peered into the gloomy, dust-hazed interior. Children were crawling in the aisle, sobbing with fear. Mrs. Marcella Platt was crawling right along with them, her voice a balm.

"Police officer," Harry called out. "Where is he?"

Children stared at him, eyes wide with wonder and amazement. Mrs. Platt almost cried with relief and stabbed a finger right at him.

"Went out the door . . . right where you're standing."

Harry turned quickly away from the door and ran toward the ramshackle wooden buildings of the quarry works.

The Luger made a sharp, barking sound as the killer fired from behind the corner of a shed. The bullets spurted dust at Harry's feet and he dove for the ground, rolling with the impact, but he was returning the fire before his body had stopped moving. The magnum splintered wood from the shed and the killer raced across a stretch of open ground toward the shadows of a tall, corrugated iron structure that housed the conveyor system. Harry squeezed off one careful shot but the killer was running a crazy, broken pattern and the shot went in the right place but at the wrong time.

Harry spat a curse and stumbled to his feet. He crossed the open ground firing as he came, aiming low for the shadows of the open-sided building, hoping to pin the killer down. He made it as far as the knife line of shadow before a bullet whip cracked past his head. He caught a fleeting glimpse of the killer as he raced toward a long narrow tunnel that sliced a hundred yards through a hill to the quarry. Harry braced himself against a post and sent a round after him. He saw the killer fall but felt sure that he hadn't hit him.

"All right, you bastard. Play possum." He ducked past the whirling conveyor-belt machinery and into the tunnel, keeping close to the side so that his body wouldn't be silhouetted against the light. He held his gun low, probing the darkness, tensed for a shadow to move.

The Luger flamed, the sound of the shot booming through the tunnel. Harry fired to the right of the gun flash and the bullet ricocheted off the hard-packed floor.

"Missed me . . . pig."

The Luger flashed again, far down near the circle of yellow light that marked the exit. Harry flung himself to one side and fell onto the conveyor. The broad canvas belt creaked and rattled on its bearings, moving toward the quarry faster than a man could walk. Harry lay prone on it, riding it into the sunlight, coming out of the tunnel in time to see the killer sprinting past mounds of crushed sandstone. A few workmen scattered, dropping their shovels as the killer flourished his Luger at them. Harry raced after him, gaining ground. The killer vaulted a low wire fence and dropped from view behind a screen of tall grass.

Harry went under the wire and wormed his way on his belly through the grass. The ground fell away twenty feet from the fence, sloping down into an irrigation ditch. A ribbon of water moved sluggishly through bulrush and hyacinth. Standing in the water, waiting for him, stood the killer—and a ten-year-old boy, the boy held tightly in the crook of his left arm.

"Come on down, *cop!*"

Harry got slowly to his feet, keeping his gun leveled. The killer grinned at him, then laughed in wild triumph. "A dumb kid, right? Fishing! In a goddamn ditch!" The laughter left his voice as he brought the Luger up and rested the tip of the barrel in the boy's ear. "Drop your gun, Callahan. Drop it slow and easy or I'll blow his brains right out the side of his head."

Mother of God, pray for me. Harry fired, not aiming, trusting on twenty years of faithful attendance at the firing range to guide the direction of his arm. The killer spun on his heels, the Luger flying from his hand, blood spraying from his left shoulder a scant inch from where the boy's head had been. The boy fell into the rushes and cowered there, whimpering. The killer staggered to his knees in the shallow water and groped for his gun in the thick weeds.

Harry walked slowly toward him and then stopped, watching the man's desperate search for the Luger.

"Tell me. Was it five times I shot or was it six? And if five, do I keep one under the hammer? Regulations say no, but you know how it is. Funny . . . it always comes down to the same question—are you feeling lucky, punk?"

The killer threw his body backward, the Luger in his hand, firing as he lifted it out of the grass.

BLAM

The magnum shell caught him in the chest and the Luger kept coming up and up and up . . . pointing to the sky as he fell back into the shallow ditch, his eyes sightless, staring at the stars that were there, the stars that were burnt out by the sun. A thin stream of scarlet flowed into the water and drifted gently through the weed.

Harry looked down at him for a long time. It was

over and he hadn't done a damn thing right. Scorpio lay dead in a ditch, but he had placed a dozen innocent lives in jeopardy to put him there. William T. Rothko would have a field day with *this* report.

Harry slipped the magnum into his holster. If he were smart, he would toss it into the water and his badge right after it. Toss it away before they took it from him. He knew this, but then if he had been really smart he wouldn't have become a cop in the first place.

He sat down in the tall grass, feeling suddenly very weary. From far away he could hear the sound of sirens coming down the quarry road and he waited for them to come nearer. Tomorrow was another day—and he would wait for that, too.

GENERAL FICTION

Δ	042607114X	Cyril Abraham **THE ONEDIN LINE: THE SHIPMASTER**	80p
Δ	0426132661	**THE ONEDIN LINE: THE IRON SHIPS**	80p
Δ	042616184X	**THE ONEDIN LINE: THE HIGH SEAS**	80p
Δ	0426172671	**THE ONEDIN LINE: THE TRADE WINDS**	80p
Δ	0352304006	**THE ONEDIN LINE: THE WHITE SHIPS**	90p
	0352302550	Spiro T. Agnew **THE CANFIELD DECISION**	£1.25*
	0352302690	Lynne Reid Banks **MY DARLING VILLAIN**	85p
Δ	0352301481	Michael J. Bird **WHO PAYS THE FERRYMAN?**	85p
Δ	0352302747	**THE APHRODITE INHERITANCE**	85p
	0352302712	Judy Blume **FOREVER**	75p*
	0352303441	Barbara Brett **BETWEEN TWO ETERNITIES**	75p*
	0352302003	Jeffrey Caine **HEATHCLIFF**	75p
	0352304987	Ramsey Campbell **THE DOLL WHO ATE HIS MOTHER**	75p*
Δ	0426187539	R. Chetwynd-Hayes **DOMINIQUE**	75p
Δ	0352395621	Jackie Collins **THE STUD**	75p
	0352300701	**LOVEHEAD**	75p
	0352398663	**THE WORLD IS FULL OF DIVORCED WOMEN**	75p
Δ	0352398752	**THE WORLD IS FULL OF MARRIED MEN**	75p
	0426163796	Catherine Cookson **THE GARMENT**	70p
	0426163524	**HANNAH MASSEY**	70p
	0426163605	**SLINKY JANE**	70p
	0352302194	Tony Curtis **KID ANDREW CODY AND JULIE SPARROW**	95p*
	0352396113	Robertson Davies **FIFTH BUSINESS**	95p*
	0352395281	**THE MANTICORE**	£1.25*
Δ	0352396881	Alexander Edwards **A STAR IS BORN**	60p*

† For sale in Britain and Ireland only
*Not for sale in Canada.
♦ Film & TV tie-ins

Wyndham Books are obtainable from many booksellers and newsagents. If you have any difficulty please send purchase price plus postage on the scale below to:

Wyndham Cash Sales,
P.O. Box 11,
Falmouth,
Cornwall

OR

Star Book Service,
G.P.O. Box 29,
Douglas,
Isle of Man,
British Isles

While every effort is made to keep prices low, it is sometimes necessary to increase prices at short notice. Wyndham Books reserve the right to show new retail prices on covers which may differ from those advertised in the text or elsewhere.

Postage and Packing Rate
U.K.
One book 25p plus 10p per copy for each additional book ordered to a maximum charge of £1.05

B.F.P.O. and Eire
One book 25p plus 10p per copy for the next 8 books and thereafter 5p per book. Overseas 40p for the first book and 12p per copy for each additional book.